T0069336

**Also by Max Byrd**

*The Sixth Conspirator: A Novel*

a novel

# Max Byrd

PERMUTED
PRESS

A PERMUTED PRESS BOOK

ISBN: 978-1-68261-921-6
ISBN (eBook): 978-1-68261-922-3

Pont Neuf
© 2020 by Max Byrd
All Rights Reserved

Cover art by Cody Corcoran
Interior layout by Sarah Heneghan, sarah-heneghan.com

This book is a work of historical fiction. All incidents, dialogue, and characters aside from the actual historical figures are products of the author's imagination. While they are based around real people, any incidents or dialogue involving the historical figures are fictional and are not intended to depict actual events or commentary. In all other respects, any resemblance to actual persons, living or dead, events, or locales is purely coincidental.

No part of this book may be reproduced, stored in a retrieval system, or transmitted by any means without the written permission of the author and publisher.

**PERMUTED**
PRESS

Permuted Press, LLC
New York • Nashville
permutedpress.com

Published in the United States of America

Quamquam animus meminisse horret,
luctuque refugit,
Incipiam.

Virgil, *Aeneid*, II, 12-13

"Although my mind shudders at the memory and
shrinks back from the pain of it, I will begin."

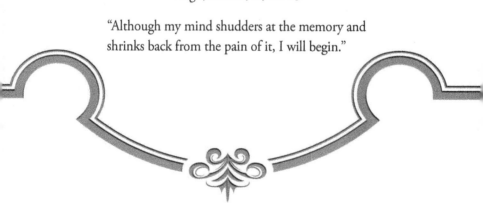

# Table of Contents

# Prologue

## December 5, 1945

The City of Light was, as usual, black as a hearse.

To be fair, here and there along the rue Daunou you could see a yellowish glow behind a curtain. Down an alley, the red tip of a whore's cigarette floated eerily in the shadows. And of course, like a candle in a cave, at number five there was the single streetlamp jerry-rigged outside Harry's Bar, undoubtedly powered by a black-market generator. Electricity in Paris was still limited to six hours a day, and it was now well past the cutoff hour of ten o'clock.

Because he was either nervous or angry, or both, Adams's mind jumped about disjointedly.

They had both hated Harry's Bar when they were in Paris. Harry's smug little leather-bottomed hideaway bar, haunted by desk-bound generals and sour-faced expats. Along with the Ritz, it was supposed to be Hemingway's favorite bar. Adams had met Hemingway and he didn't like him. He'd never met a soldier who liked Hemingway.

Ahead of him, Annabella Sidonie March stepped expertly over what Adams assumed was, in one of her jokey expressions, "dog evidence." He paused and looked carefully into the darkness behind him. Nobody. After the length of one quick, cold breath

1

he followed her around the corner onto the place Vendôme, where electricity rationing had been relaxed for the big international hotels, and he blinked at the sudden dazzling glare of the Ritz marquee. To his right, headlights from a procession of cars swept like a school of fish toward the Opéra.

Then it was all black again until they reached the rue de Rivoli. Here, another hotel was also lit, and Adams could see a woman in the lobby hanging strips of tinfoil over a Christmas tree. Squinting, he recognized them as the radio-foiling ribbons that American bombers had dropped over Paris before the Liberation, and he wondered who in the world would have thought to collect such things—trinket-hungry kids, maybe. Only the French would think to turn them into ornaments.

It had been raining earlier, but Paris was a city that liked to change her mind. Now the rain was metamorphosing into fluttering white moths, snowflakes that tumbled through the darkness and smacked wet and cold into his face. Up ahead, Annie March, who'd had the sense to wear a hat, was saying something in her superb French to the gendarme at the Tuileries Garden steps. He moved aside with a Gallic flourish of his cape, and a minute later they were tramping across the big open space toward the river.

Here the snow had already started to stick. The garden's dead grass shivered under a thin coat of it. Close to the southern wall the wind swooped and kicked up miniature white whirlwinds that danced a few yards and collapsed. Adams's mind jumped again. In the Ardennes, when German shells fell short of the foxholes, the snow had done the same thing; it had puffed and climbed to its feet and spun wildly toward them like gyrating ghosts, like an army of spectres.

*Angry*, he decided. He was *angry*, not *nervous*.

They reached the Pont des Arts, which, like all bridges, connected two worlds. Without streetlamps he could sense more than he could see the ragged line of buildings that blocked the inner world of the Left Bank from the Right Bank's view and guarded its secrets. He had been angry with Shaw for months—angry, furious, bitter—a thesaurus of disappointment—*saeva indignatio* as the Latin-spouting son of a bitch would probably say—angry even before the Ardennes. By October he had almost managed to tamp it down and forget. Then Annie March called.

He'd been angry with Annie, too.

He had no idea where she was taking him, but now the quai du Louvre curved gently north and they turned onto the Pont Neuf, the "New Bridge," which every tourist knew was actually the oldest bridge in Paris. Back in the sixteenth century Henri IV had intended it to be a commercial bridge for wagons and horses. But you cannot keep thoughts of war from regal minds very long, Adams thought, so every fifty feet or so the king had added semi-circular bastions that projected outward from the balustrades, just as they would from the wall of a fort.

Shaw wouldn't like a fort. Too defensive for Shaw.

Annie March chose a bastion on the right, about sixty yards in, and turned around to face downstream. Adams stamped his shoes in the snow and looked back in the direction of the Louvre. Still nobody. A car with yellow cat's eye headlights swished past. Then there was nothing, no light, no sound at all except the hiss of the snow and the wind and, sixty feet below, the ancient river muttering to itself.

He held up his watch to the nonexistent light and guessed it was past eleven. A snowflake fell on the dial. There were no twin snowflakes. No two snowflakes were alike, no two moments of time. No two people. There were no twins in nature.

Annie looked sharply to her right.

"He's coming," she said.

# PART ONE

## Normandy and Paris
## Summer 1944

# One

"COLONEL SCRIPTURE," DRAWLED AN ELEGANT BRYN MAWR voice, "is the turd that won't flush."

A yard or two in front of them, windblown and out of focus, Martha Gellhorn automatically assumed the lead and started along the dirt road, well to the left of the line of ambulances and jeeps clattering up the hill. Annabella March—who had been plain "Annie" since a legendary tantrum in the second grade—wiped sweat from her face and saw an olive-green shirt with fancy black epaulets, a steel pot helmet fringed with blonde hair, and the perfect bottom for which Martha Gellhorn was hated by two-thirds of the other women.

They were in Normandy under a hot June sun, almost three weeks after the D-Day landings, and they had just scrambled out of the First Army ordnance truck assigned to transport them. And now, having passed through a somber chaos of idyllic French farmland clawed to tatters by guns and tanks, they found themselves ten miles southeast of Utah Beach, five miles behind the actual fighting, trudging toward the entrance to the First Army, 44th Evacuation Hospital, which was going to be their home for the next three days.

The 44th was situated, like most field hospitals, in a pasture. The pasture itself, smallish and on a slant, was surrounded by a protective wall of dark, dusty apple trees, low brush, and the swayback remains of an ancient stonewall. In addition to the hospital, the pasture hosted a dozen or so cows, wandering free at the moment, who (unknown to themselves) were there to walk over any mines the retreating Germans might have left behind.

It was because of the mines—and an all-purpose masculine irritability—that the offending Colonel Scripture had had them stopped right at the landing beach and ordered back to England. When they talked their way around that somehow, he had them arrested and brought to his command post in Bayeux. There, grimly furious, he banged his desk and railed against "goddamned reporter women," until Martha waved in his face some kind of *passe-partout* from (she said) General Omar Bradley, an old family friend, and all the steam went out of Colonel Scripture.

Annie assumed the pass was a forgery. Martha was a gifted writer of fiction—"A born liar, my dear"—and in her own words, she had morals, but not scruples.

Their party included a non-com escort from Pittsburgh, glad to be doing something other than fighting Germans out in the murderous Normandy hedgerows, and three extremely nervous, newly assigned army nurses who kept to themselves. While the sentry checked their papers at the gate, Annie studied the cows. She half expected to see one explode.

But the cows grazed peacefully, plump and intact, so she turned and listened to the distant sound of big guns, a steady thump-thump-thump, like a pulse.

THE COLONEL IN CHARGE OF THE 44TH EVAC WAS NO HAPPIER TO see them than Colonel Scripture had been. But he looked at the *passe-partout*, blew stoically on his moustache, and signed something on a clipboard.

They were to bunk in Nurses' Tent Number Five, which was the last in the file of tents closest to the apple trees. When they peeked in, they saw it had trampled grass for a floor, four ranks of field cots and footlockers for furniture, and a liberated rocking chair with a liberated silk cushion for a touch of elegance. A clothesline hung with women's unmentionables stretched over the cots, kept out of sight that way from the presumably excitable men hurrying by outside. An arrow on a pole pointed toward the women's latrine, a ditch fifty yards away, behind an apple tree.

"I'm going to go pick an apple," Martha said dryly, and set off toward the latrine.

Annie sat down on the rocking chair and cleaned her glasses again. She was also a "goddam reporter woman," just like Martha Gellhorn. They both wore drab olive field clothes and steel helmets, clunked about in regulation army boots, and displayed a billiard green shoulder patch bordered in bright yellow that said "U.S. War Correspondent." The chief difference (beside the perfect bottom) was that Martha wrote for the prestigious *Collier's Magazine* and the still grander *New York Times*, while Annie was accredited only to the profoundly inconsequential British edition of *Vogue*. The other difference, of course, was that Martha was married to Ernest Hemingway, though the loving couple hadn't seen each other in months, and each was known to spit sulfur when the other was mentioned.

Being linked with Martha had its advantages. Their new colonel was apparently a literary man. When he learned who Martha was, he sent a lieutenant around to give them a tour of the hospital, before the heaviest load of wounded came in at dusk.

The lieutenant was named Lambert. He was not a literary man. He limped, he spoke with a vowel-flattening Oklahoma accent, and he guided them about with undisguised impatience. He also wore a very different shoulder patch, the Screaming Eagle's Head of the 101st Airborne Division. In the bright sun, shading her eyes, it took Annie too long to see that his right trouser leg was cut off at the ankle and showed six inches of a blood-soaked bandage. Another, cleaner bandage showed where a fist-sized part of his neck had been scooped out raw like a hollow moon. When Martha asked how he had been wounded, he stared at her and said nothing.

The tour started at the central gate, where they had come in. Lambert leaned against a jeep and told them to watch. They stood and listened to muffled voices behind them, truck engines, cows. Distant guns drummed softly, like surf heard over a hill. Then an ambulance suddenly swung off the main road and roared uphill toward the gate. Spraying dirt and rocks and stampeding the cows, it fishtailed to a halt just in front of them. Annie saw its front doors slam open. Two men scrambled to the back. A litter slid down, and shouting soldiers swarmed out of the hospital tents. Four of them grabbed the corners of the litter and trotted off toward a tent marked in great white letters, "Surgery." Under the blanket she glimpsed a boy's face torn into curling strips of white and pink flesh, as if it had just been raked with meathooks. Lambert grabbed her elbow, not gently, and pulled her away. Her eyes began to water, and she felt…forty hours ago she had been dancing in a nightclub in London…Annabella March had no idea what she felt. It was a Just War.

"Only trouble with these people," Lambert said, his first and last purely personal remark, "these doctors and nurses, they don't *hate* enough."

All the hospital tents were in street-like rows, twelve of them, arranged in the rigid grid pattern that the army used to impose its will on the undulating landscape. From the outside they looked the same—sixty-two feet long, thirty feet wide, olive drab like everything else, with ten-foot-high walls and sloping roofs. A red cross in a white circle was painted on each roof. On the ground, white tape marked paths and entrances for the blackout hours. They were humped up by poles at both ends, so that at a distance they resembled a herd of dark green dromedaries.

But inside, each one was different. In the "Shock" tent Lambert showed them perhaps twenty or twenty-five soldiers lying silently on cots. It was too hot for blankets, but most of them were covered with sheets. Some stared at the dark canvas roof. Some had plasma flasks dripping liquid into outstretched arms. Some had oxygen tubes. Near the entrance flap a soldier, not obviously wounded, sat up and smoked a cigarette while a sergeant knelt beside the cot and talked to him.

"Seeing if he's faking it," Lambert said and left them to think that over.

They looked into other tents ("Burn" ward, surgeons' prep tent, medical supply tent), and ventured as far as they were allowed into the "Surgery" tent, where six different operating tables appeared to be in constant use. In a laundry hamper, amputated arms waited for incineration.

Martha had seen dead and mangled bodies in the Spanish Civil War and earlier in this war with the Allies in Italy. Martha was her usual cool and contained and unreachable self. But Annie had never seen anything worse than a scraped knee until she stepped off the landing craft at Utah Beach. Instinctively, she retreated from the sight of so much pain and, like the good student she had always been, took refuge behind words and numbers, a wall of abstractions. She took out her notebook: "There are thirty-seven doctors assigned to each Evac Hospital," she wrote carefully as Lambert talked, "fifty-one nurses, 318 enlisted men and non-coms, 434 beds."

About five o'clock, as the coastal winds began to pull the heat down, Lambert left them at the Quartermaster's tent, where they were to draw their gear.

Martha went in first, grabbed two neatly folded clean blankets and a tin mess kit and exited fast. Annie took her blankets, then paused to look at a cardboard box overflowing like a rummage sale bin with miscellaneous clothing, caps, shirts, gun belts, eyeglasses, all kinds of personal gear.

"They get evack'd to England," the clerk said. "They leave a lot of shit behind, pardon my French. You need something?"

Annie shook her head.

"War Correspondent," the clerk read from her patch, interested. "We had an AP photographer here last week, got his foot blown off, so away he goes to England. He left this if you want it."

Automatically, Annie started to shake her head again, but then, recognizing the brand of the camera, she frowned. It was the black, boxy kind her father had brought home from the Paris World's Fair in 1937, a foreign make. It came with a leather case and strap, a flashbulb attachment, and a green musette bag full of film.

In the first of the four moments that would utterly destroy her moral universe, she picked it up.

# Two

THE CAMERA WAS A ROLLEIFLEX 35 MM FLASH, THE SAME KIND
Annie would learn that the famous war photographer Robert
Capa used. She remembered vaguely how to operate it. Her father,
given to intense but fleeting enthusiasms, had spent three or four
months photographing her and her mother and, briefly, the flowers in their garden. Then the camera had joined the fly-fishing
gear, the sketchbooks, the broken ukulele, the countless other discarded gadgets in the attic that were mute evidence of his restless
personality. ("Your father has a mind like a pinwheel," her mother
had said.)

After a hurried dinner with the nurses, Annie sat on her cot
in their tent and by the light of a Dietz lantern spent the rest of
the night fiddling with its levers and lenses. In the morning she
went out with her camera and found, to her amazement, that it
served everywhere as a kind of "Open Sesame."

In the "Belly Wound" tent, which had been off-limits the day
before, no one paid her the slightest attention, and she took a
series of surreal photographs of the interior, which looked like a
jungle of banyan trees—dozens and dozens of rubber tubes dropping from the ceiling in a thick swaying maze, delivering plasma

or blood. Every patient had a tube inserted in his nostril and another in his wound, and sometimes two or three others inexplicably protruded from a leg.

In the "Burn" tent she photographed a line of ghostly mummies—human forms wrapped in huge, thick white bandages, some from head to toe. One GI motioned her over—she could only see his mouth and one eye—and asked her to take his picture so he could see how funny he looked. She took it out of focus, deliberately, because "funny" was nothing like the word she would have used. Another talking mouth told her he had been burned when his "Ronson" went up—an obliging nurse translated: Sherman tanks used gasoline, not diesel fuel like the German tanks. When a shell hit a Sherman it went up in flames like a Ronson cigarette lighter. "They like to make jokes," the nurse said, "goddamn them."

At the "Surgery" tent, likewise off-limits the day before, she picked up a surgical mask and walked in with her camera. Nobody bothered to look up and she began to take systematic photographs of the surgeons at work, asking permission if she wanted to use the flash. The surgeons ignored her, except for one who was probing shrapnel out of somebody's pulsating lungs. He asked her what exposure he should use, if he wanted to take some pictures himself. He gestured at the brilliant surgical lights that kept ruining his own photographs. A wounded German was carried in and laid out carefully on an operating table. Another German POW, really a boy of fifteen or sixteen, stood over his head and translated for the surgeon. "They get the same treatment as our boys," a nurse said, and added like the first nurse, "goddamn them."

"Can I take his picture?"

"Over my dead body."

# Pont Neuf

Annie finished a carton of film and stepped outside, into harsh sunlight and a vague, cloudless, entirely indifferent sky. She took off what Martha called her "old lady specs," wiped them clean and put them back on, and the sky came into focus.

When you looked through glasses' lenses, she thought, the world came clearer, closer. She hefted the Rolleiflex and ran the strap over her shoulder.

But when you looked through the camera lens, nothing came closer. Somehow the camera put a merciful distance between yourself and the blood and the mutilated lungs, the white bones and the charred flesh. You didn't hear the guns and the groans and the wheezing pump of the respirator. You were like the dispassionate surgeon. You thought only about the abstract technical challenge of taking a good picture. Which made it all the more surprising to find that she was crying.

# ℑhree

MARTHA GELLHORN WAS AN ENIGMA WRAPPED IN A RIDDLE inside a mystery.

She was thirty-five, ten years older than Annie, and from the moment they met by accident in the lobby of the Dorchester Hotel, a fascinated Annie had made a study of her. In letters to her mother she listed the bewildering, contradictory personality traits that made Martha so bedeviling. (All personalities are contradictory, her mother wrote back.)

For one thing, Martha was ferociously independent. She disliked authority of all kinds and regarded military regulations as either insult or joke. Yet despite that, she had married the hyper-bullying Ernest Hemingway, whose bare-chested photograph was once on the cover of *Esquire* above the caption, "America's Manliest Man." (She showed Annie an angry telegram he had sent her in London, demanding that she come back home—"Are you a war correspondent, or wife in my bed?")

For another thing, she was a self-described "feminist" and loudly denounced the army's restrictions on women journalists with a mixture of irony and arrogance that infuriated the Colonel Scriptures of the world. She wanted to be where the shooting was,

17

not where worrywart men wanted her to be. Yet paradoxically, most of her newspaper stories, from the Spanish Civil War on, were about civilians, not soldiers.

She also disliked sex. This was more than surprising in someone of her striking good looks and history of scandalous affairs, and her bluntness about it made Annie blush. The first night in the Evac Hospital, slightly in her cups—Martha did not dislike alcohol—she told Annie that she never got any real pleasure from sex. She just didn't enjoy it. She would only sleep with Hemingway after all her excuses failed. "I always hoped it would be over quickly," she said before rolling over on her cot and beginning unglamorously to snore.

Annie lay on her back and smelled the moldy canvas of the tent roof. She heard the grind of gears and ambulance motors down the hill, the occasional squeal of tires and the shouts of panicked men who doubtless also hoped it would be over quickly. Six or seven miles away the guns thumped and paused, thumped and paused.

And then, too, Martha was an obsessive writer. This was something Annie genuinely envied. Martha lived, it seemed, for nothing but writing. She had already published five novels and a collection of short stories, not to mention hundreds of dispatches from the Spanish Civil War. She wrote so well and so quickly that *Collier's* had put her at the top of their masthead as War Correspondent, until Hemingway complained and replaced her. Maxwell Perkins was her adoring editor at Scribner's. Eleanor Roosevelt praised her books in the newspapers. She had gone to bed with H.G. Wells in London and then—Annie shook her head in admiration—brazenly asked him to critique her prose. And of course—it all came full circle—there was that most literary of marriages to the great stud bull of American letters, who also (Annie surmised) envied and feared her.

Some of the nurses were whispering. In a nearby tent a man screamed in pain. Annie fumbled under the cot and touched her camera. Her finger curled around the shutter lever, like a trigger. She wasn't like Martha. She wasn't obsessive enough. And she really wasn't a very good writer. Maybe a picture would in fact be worth a thousand words.

In the dark she frowned at the cliché. Out loud she muttered the infuriating advice of her first editor. "Don't get it right, Annabella. *Get it written.*"

"Is Mr. Hemingway with you, may I ask?" The exophthalmic British major on Martha's left tugged at his necktie and gave an encouraging nod.

"I'm told he's finally come ashore," she said coolly, "now that the fighting's farther inland and it's safe."

"Oh no, surely," the major protested. Then to cover all possibilities, "Surely not."

It was Martha's glamour, of course, that had gotten them out of the Evac Hospital and three miles closer to the front. It had also gotten them invited to this particular officers' mess tent, an Allied communications command post attached to the Twenty-Ninth Infantry Division of Omar Bradley's First Army. Or more accurately, it was the pop-eyed major's curiosity. In peacetime he was a sub-editor on *The Daily Telegraph* and a would-be novelist. Annie was half afraid he was going to reach into his jacket and pull out a manuscript for Martha to vet.

"A fête worse than death," Martha said in answer to another question. "K rations. That's all we ate in Italy. I would have killed for some pasta."

They were ranged along a battered metal table under the ubiquitous green canvas of a military tent, listening to rain, listening to the distant crack of small arms fire, and eating an officers' meal

19

of red-eye gravy, lamb chops and Norman cider. Annie took in Martha's inimitable patter with only half an ear. After ten days of traveling with her, she had already heard most of Martha's stories. And besides, what Annie wanted was not another round of Hemingway gossip, but a look at the GIs actually under fire, the lean, gaunt, incredibly filthy and unshaven young men who were only a few miles away, tangled in the hedgerows, dying by inches.

"I only tried the chocolate bar once," Martha was saying. "It tasted like a slice of linoleum."

Annie had nothing like Martha's imagination. She was an only child, but sometimes she pictured herself as the sister of a dozen coltish, adoring brothers, who were now out there crawling through the mud while she stayed guiltily out of range, talking about food.

"Did you know," Martha asked the table, "that General Bradley has his own personal ice-cream making machine? Goes with him everywhere. I wanted Annie to take a photograph of it. What did they tell you, Annie?"

Annie hated being dragged into Martha's act. "His staff said it was classified information."

The younger officers laughed uneasily, the colonel at the end of the table grimaced. Annie stood up and excused herself and went outside to stand in the rain.

"She's our idealist," she heard Martha say as she left. "A regular cheerleader."

"She's very pretty," someone said, "despite the glasses. She has that cute little overbite."

"She writes human interest stories," Martha said with the faintest hint of condescension. "Uplifting, patriotic stories. She doesn't know yet," she added, pursing her lips to signal quotation,

"'Life is a tragedy to those who feel, a comedy to those who think.'"

"Shakespeare," said the major, wrong as usual.

BY THE FIRST WEEK IN JULY, MARTHA HAD GROWN SO FRUS-
trated that abruptly—Martha did many things abruptly—she
pulled out of Normandy and returned to London. From London she hitched a ride with a friendly RAF pilot to Naples and
rejoined her old unit, where she felt there would be fewer lim-
itations on her movements. But before she left, she sent Annie
a copy of a letter to Eisenhower blasting the army's regulations
about women reporters, who were not, she scolded the Supreme
Commander, "china dolls to be wrapped in swaddling." Then
cheerfully mixing her metaphors, she added that his policy had
turned them all into "lepers."

On her own, Annie suddenly felt freer. At Carentan, she
found a camera supply store that had miraculously survived
three days of bombardment and house-to-house fighting. She
bought a big bag of Rolleiflex film and, with no orders, no
papers, no masculine permission whatsoever, thumbed her
way twenty miles east and talked her way into the battalion
aid station of one Colonel Robert Cole, a baby-faced, twenty-
nine-year-old paratrooper she had danced with a lifetime ago
in London.

Cole's battalion was too busy fighting to pay attention to her.
She tagged along with artillery observers and ammunition carri-
ers, farther and farther into the hedgerows, sometimes crawling
on the wet Norman earth no more than half a mile behind the
medics, sometimes being unceremoniously ordered to carry a
message back to the command post or question a Frenchman.
On the second of August she crept close enough to see the faces
of German soldiers as they peered through the trees. "I have

heard the charming sound of bullets," she wrote Martha, quoting George Washington.

The funny thing about the camera was that it often seemed to stop the war altogether, or at least put it in slow motion. Over and over, a GI—one of her fantasy brothers, some twenty year-old kid with an M-1 and a peach fuzz beard, would call out as he ran past—"Hey, lady, take my picture! Put it in the paper!" Outside Caen, as huge B-17 bombers blackened the sky, obliterating the city, a group of Polish POWs motioned her over. They were sitting on the ground in their raincoats, their hands on top of their heads, grinning—their war was over—"Come take our picture!" they shouted in comically bad French. They asked if she would kiss them, or marry them, or just let them smell her hair.

Week after week through all of July, Colonel Cole and his boy soldiers advanced, yard by bloody yard, through the hedge-rows—hedgerows that were not in fact hedges, but thick, wildly overgrown mounds of earth dating back to Roman times, when farmers built them to keep cattle in. Their impossibly tangled vegetation blocked jeeps, half-tracks, even tanks. No one could see through it or over it. Twice, the boys told her, the colonel himself had led desperate bayonet charges over the hedgerows and into the ditches behind them. It was like fighting in a maze, they said.

Annie tried to picture the mild-mannered, deeply religious colonel driving an eight-inch steel blade through the throat of yet another screaming, unshaven boy, and her eyes filled with generous tears. And yet, despite that image, a feeling of patriotism welled up inside her. She loved the soldiers around her more and more. She loved their gaiety, their shyness, their lanky American bodies offered up in bloody sacrifice on a for-eign altar. Martha had told her that Eros and Thanatos, Love and Death, stalked the fields of war, and Annie began to think she understood, though, of course, like all idealists, she misunderstood what was meant by love.

# ℱour

THE FIRST PHOTOGRAPH ANNIE SOLD TO *VOGUE* WAS TAKEN IN the cathedral city of Chartres, fifty-six miles southwest of Paris.

It happened this way.

She had seen Chartres once before, nine years earlier, when her father, recovering from what would be his penultimate stroke, took her out of school and brought her to Europe for a tour of medieval churches—the latest and almost the last of his serial enthusiasms. What she remembered was the low, flat farmland that the train from Paris clattered through, then the muddy brown Eure River, then the two great cloud-piercing spires of the cathedral—she didn't wear glasses then—visible from the train twenty minutes before they rolled to a halt at the station.

Now, sixteen years later, mid-August, 1944, the great spires were still visible from miles away. But this time they pierced a different kind of cloud, the wildly gyrating blossoms of black and white smoke thrown up by Allied artillery, shrouding the city. And this time she saw them, not from a train, but from the bouncing, unpadded shotgun seat of a Third Army munitions supply truck. She wiped her specs and looked over her shoulder. Behind them, like a gigantic, articulated mechanical snake, trucks and tanks and jeeps coiled in an endless olive-green line, free at last of the Norman hedgerows, lashing their way angrily across France toward the Rhine. (General Bradley had named this "Operation Cobra.") Overhead the bombers droned and stung. The smoke twisted and climbed, closer and closer every moment to the spires.

Annie had adored the cathedral, and so had her father. Before the trip they had gone over books about Gothic architecture together and made lists of things to notice, recondite architectural terms to remember—nave, clerestory, tympanum, archivolt. In his small, precise hand, her father drew a chart of the famous stained-glass windows, and they had cheerfully practiced leaning against his study wall and turning each other into flying buttresses.

But now she was horrified to learn that General Patton, in his usual state of unslaked fury, certain there were German snipers in the bell tower, had ordered his artillery to reduce the great, irreplaceable cathedral to pious rubble.

A logistics officer in the XX Corps, Colonel Welborn B. Griffith of Quanah, Texas, not a Catholic, not even especially religious, found himself unexpectedly overcome with outrage. He was determined that American barbarians were not going to be the ones who destroyed one of the spiritual wonders of the world.

On his own, he ordered his driver to cut through the American forward lines and, with crazy Texas bravery, the two of them drove straight into the city, under constant fire from astonished German infantry, until they reached the west portal. There, Colonel Griffith jumped out of his jeep and ran into the nave. Then he climbed the bell tower, .45 in hand, and searched it up and down. No Germans. He got back to his jeep and on his radio, on his own authority, stopped the artillery fire. Patton snarled himself into one of his fits, but six hours later, when the Germans finally started to pull out of Chartres, the 750-year-old spires were still standing, undamaged, still pointing skyward.

Annie arrived at the same spot at dusk. She leapt down from her truck and fished out her camera from her rucksack. On the right-hand steps of the portal, under the wary gaze of a row of carved saints, two dirty, rumpled, unshaven GIs cradled their rifles and watched as a white-haired priest carrying a golden crucifix shuffled toward the center door. Annie's camera caught the soldiers staring at the priest, whose black robe billowed behind him like a filling sail, while the Virgin's face floated in the twilight just above them. As she clicked the shutter, the setting sun drew a sash of light across the ancient gray stone. It was a dramatic photograph, bold with irony and contrast, and completely an amateur's luck. Her editor paid her five pounds for it.

THE NEXT DAY SHE SOLD A SECOND, BETTER PHOTOGRAPH.

It happened *this* way.

On the day after the Germans left Chartres, Annie found herself bunked in a hotel in the city center, sharing a room with two plucky and excitable nurses from Shaker Heights, Ohio.

How long had they been here?

Two months, they said, and why didn't she write a story about *them*? "Buckeye babes in the war," they joked, "bandaging up old Europe"—what could be better?

"And you can tell them back home that I love it!" the nearer one said. She was wearing a red bra and men's khaki trousers a size too big and she bent over a bucket of cold water and started to wash her hair, still chattering. "The bad stuff you expect, the wounds and the hospitals and the amputations, but it's still fascinating. Tell them it's like being in the fucking *Iliad*! Pardon my French."

"That's not French," her friend said. "She's been around too many fucking soldiers." She gave Annie's chest a critical look. "You need to do this, Annie," she said, then threw back her shoulders and began to rotate them, chanting under her breath, *"You must, you must,/You must increase your bust!"*

Annoyed, Annie smiled. But she straightened her back all the same.

"Three times a day," the first nurse laughed, "just like sex."

"Fucking sex," her friend said, and they both bared perfect white American teeth in irresistible grins. Well, why *not* write a story about them? Annie thought. And why not reread the fucking *Iliad* while you're at it?

She set up her camera and posed them on the balcony. Through the viewfinder they looked like a pair of fresh-faced Rapunzels in army fatigues, about to lower their tresses to a squad of Prince Charmings.

But the street below suddenly erupted into shouting and cheers and any thought of Prince Charming was blown away by the uproar. All three peered down to see a wild and growing commotion, a mass—an impromptu *parade*—of civilians so loud and raucous that Annie turned her camera away from the nurses and started to galumph down the stairs for a better story.

When she reached the sidewalk and shot out the door, she found herself swept into a mob of clamoring men and women, some shaking their fists, some jeering, everyone shouting, *howling* in furious, incoherent French. Just ahead of her, being viciously pushed and slapped at random, stumbled six or eight young Frenchwomen dressed incongruously in colorful floral-patterned summer dresses. Their heads were completely shaven. One of them was smirking. The others looked stunned, cataleptic.

*"Horizontales!"* somebody told Annie and spat at the nearest girl.

"They slept with the Boches!" somebody screamed in her ear, "*Whores, whores, whores!*"

By now Annie was at the very head of the crowd and because she was wearing her steel helmet and her correspondent's uniform, the French took her for a soldier. In the noise and confusion, a man in a baker's apron shook her hand, an old woman grabbed her ears and kissed her on both cheeks. Annie lifted her camera and tried to sight it.

The first three girls walked stoically toward her through a gauntlet of waving arms and curses. Spittle flowed down their faces, spots of blood glistened on their scalps where the *tondeur* had wielded his razor too roughly. Their heads were pale white knobs in the sunshine. The girl in the middle had a swastika drawn in lipstick on her forehead and she held a small crying baby in her arms.

Annie peered through the viewfinder and caught for the readers of *Vogue* their first image of the punishment French civilians would deal out for the rest of the war to women who had collaborated horizontally with the Germans. Her editor passed it on to the Associated Press and paid her another five pounds.

LATER, IN A DARK CAFÉ SHE DRANK TWO QUICK GLASSES OF WARM vermouth and tried to stop her hands from trembling. She was a war correspondent, she told herself, she had already seen dead bodies, mangled bodies, too many horrors. But this, she thought—*women, girls.* Self-consciously, she ran her fingers through her own black hair. Then she pulled out her notebook and, without pausing for writer's panic, began to scribble copy to go along with the photograph.

To block out feelings, pedantic facts were almost as good as a camera. Shaving a woman's head to shame her, she remembered, had biblical origins, though she couldn't recall the texts—Jezebel

in her fine wig? Eve's golden locks? What else? Martha had told
her that in the Spanish Civil War the Falangists shaved the heads
of women from republican families. Clearly—Annie tried for a
dispassionate and scholarly voice—the act was symbolic, meant
to tear away a woman's distinctive, seductive feature and destroy
her sexuality.

Her hands were still trembling when she tore out the pages
from her notebook and stuffed them in a courier envelope. The
French word for all this, she thought numbly, was *épuration*,
which meant "purification"—a feminine noun, of course.

After she had taken her film to the army censor and mailed it
to London, she went back onto the streets. At the square where
the women had been shaved she saw a disgusting pile of hair on
the cobblestones. Some of it was still smoldering from the mob's
self-righteous attempt to burn it. At the Mairie two of the women
she had photographed were being held in protective custody
while the magistrate decided what to do with them. And because
the French were still mistaking her for a *femme soldat*, the guards
let her in to interview them.

She found them in a locked room at the back, a nearly bare
storeroom, furnished only with three straight-backed chairs and
a dusty wooden file cabinet. The first woman was plump and
pretty, and she stared vacantly at Annie, as Martha would have
put it, like a tranced cow.

"*Vous parlez français?*" she said in surprise when Annie spoke
to her in French. "*Une Americaine?*" Then she turned her head
and closed her eyes.

The second one was the woman with the baby and the lipstick
swastika on her forehead, which was now illegible, smeared on
her skin like a crushed rose. She was older, not nearly as plump or
pretty. The sleeves of her dress had been ripped at both shoulders,

showing thin arms badly scratched and bruised. The baby slept restlessly in her arms. "*Vous parlez français couramment*," she said.

"Who were those people outside?" Annie asked. "*Resistants?*"

"You must have learned it in school," the woman said, still in French. "Some good American school, far from the war."

"In college," Annie said.

"'Those people' were my friends and neighbors," the woman said with a sad, slow smile. "I grew up with them. I was a teacher in a school. They think I disgraced France because I lived with a German soldier." The baby stirred and kicked one foot free of the swaddling, and she bent over it like a bald Madonna. "Her father. He's dead now. She looks like him." Abruptly tears came into her eyes. "I had such *beautiful* hair."

Annie looked away. Through the wall she heard voices on the street, still shouting. A fly landed on the woman's scalp and started to crawl across the stubbled white skin. She made no move to brush it away.

"His name was Phillip, and I didn't think it was wrong. He was so young, and lonely, and so very scared. I thought to myself, he *needs* me." She cradled the baby closer. "You understand that, because you're a woman," and it wasn't clear which one of them she was speaking to, Annie or the baby. Then she raised her head and looked at Annie through red, swollen eyes, with the same sad, slow smile. "That's how love always is," she said, "isn't it?"

When Annie saw her photograph in print, she went into the toilet and threw up.

# 𝔉iue

Paris was liberated by the Allies on August 25, but Annie, sick with a late summer flu and stuck in Chartres, didn't make it there until four days later.

No matter, everybody told her—the party would go on for weeks!

Certainly it was going on at the Hôtel Scribe, which the army had taken over as a residence for correspondents—"Hello, 'Sexy Specs,'" a very drunk AP reporter told her happily. "Come on over, it's like this every night!" He sloshed his drink in unsteady benediction over the journalists jammed three and four deep around the bar. A bespectacled *Life* reporter named David Schuyler, who had a cigarette dangling from his lips like Edward R. Murrow, detached himself from the scrimmage and handed her a full tumbler of scotch. It was like a "Newspaperman's Mecca," he shouted over the noise, but Annie thought it was more like the fraternity house at Dartmouth where she had once gone on a blind date. When she asked after Martha and Hemingway, Schuyler told her in disgust that Hemingway was unwilling to mingle with ordinary writers at the Scribe. Instead, he had conspicuously installed himself at the Ritz, where he held daily court to a rag-tag group of hangers-on that he called his "Irregulars." Of Martha, he said, there was no sign.

The Hôtel Scribe—perfect name for a gathering of writers—was a grand old pile of a building, just off the boulevard des Capucines on the Right Bank. It had first opened for business in 1865, named for a well-known dramatist of the day, and at the time it must have seemed like the last word in luxury. But now its handsome limestone facade was chipped and stained by bullets and shells from street fighting and the elegant lobby smelled of kerosene and gunpowder. The corridors were overflowing with stenciled crates and boxes. The basement was being used to store K rations for the soldiers and whiskey and champagne for the officers. Thanks to its enormous stock of whisky being liberated by the reporters on an hourly basis, the hotel bar was open. But the restaurant, the "Grand Café," was closed.

Annie peered into its main room, which was mostly empty and lit only by candles because there was no electricity. Not much food either, a glum waiter told her. The Germans ate it all. She took a photograph of two army majors at a table eating K rations and drinking champagne from crystal flutes.

At the mail desk she found a telegram from her editor, who reminded her pointedly that photographs of the war were all very well, but now that she was in Paris, *Vogue* readers wanted to hear about *fashion*.

Annie cringed at this. She was a professional *war* correspondent, she told herself. She had reported on field hospitals and bombing raids, and she had crawled on her hands and knees through the hedgerows of Normandy, in sight and sound of actual combat. She held out her arms and sniffed her sleeves. She had worn the same smelly khaki shirt and pants and socks—not to mention her unmentionables—for days at a time. She hadn't taken a bath in more than a week because the water in Chartres had been suddenly cut off and there was no soap. The Scribe had water, but unheated and only for twenty minutes a day, and she had arrived too late even for that. She looked at the mirror and saw that she had raccoon rings of black grease around her eyes and a neck so filthy she could almost feel her mother's knuckles in the washcloth as she scrubbed and purified her dirt-caked little girl. The girl in the mirror grinned sardonically at her. Sure, go write about fashion.

BUT TO HER SURPRISE, THERE *WAS* FASHION TO WRITE ABOUT.

Outside the Scribe the next morning she noticed broken glass everywhere, which reminded her of London after a bombing. Most of the handsome nineteenth-century buildings around the hotel were pockmarked with bullet holes or had corners or walls ripped away by artillery shells. Near the Hôtel Crillon, where the occupying German commandant had set up his headquarters, streets were blocked off and bi-lingual signs warned of booby traps. In front of the Crillon, the place de la Concorde was enclosed by barbed wire. She saw little boys playing on a burned-out car. At the corner of the rue de la Paix and the avenue de l'Opéra she came across a wrecked German tank and more little boys playing. Here and there a poster in German lettering hung limply on a lamppost, not yet torn down. A few cafés on the Champs-Elysées had put out chairs and tables, though there was precious little food to serve and only an undrinkable ersatz coffee made up, as far as she could tell, of burnt acorns and chicory. Parisians called it "Muckefuck," a sympathetic waiter explained, and she wondered whether *Vogue* would print that.

But the girls! The girls were everywhere, the most beautiful girls she had ever seen—Paris was still torn and smoking from its weeks of fighting, but wherever Annie looked, the city was dancing with white and blonde blossoms, dazzling young women in floating skirts and tiny waistlines, hair in waving curls. They rode madly up and down the city in jeeps with laughing GIs, they climbed up on the turrets of tanks and gave the soldiers flowers and kisses. As for fashion, nobody wore makeup—there had been no makeup or *couture* in the Occupation—and many blouses and skirts were un-washed and un-ironed, but worn with Parisian panache all the same. Those girls who couldn't find soap or hot water to wash their hair put on stylish turbans instead. The helpful (and now sober) David Schuyler took her to photograph the one hairdresser in Paris who could dry hair. He turned out, in the best French tradition, to have only one name, "Gervais," and he had rigged a Rube Goldberg system of stovepipes and fans to a furnace in the basement of his building. There was no coal or electricity, of course, so he had teams of boys collecting wood from the streets for the furnace and another team riding a stationary bicycle attached to a pulley to turn the fans and blow the warm air upstairs.

When she had trouble adjusting her camera to the darkness of the basement, Schuyler, who turned out to be a photographer, not a reporter, for *Life*, showed her how to adjust her focus without her glasses and work the shutter to get more light. "'More light,'" he joked, "the photographer's creed, Goethe's last words!" Afterwards, at the Scribe, he gave her another lesson in photography and then a hilarious dinner of carrot and turnip soup and champagne. They went to bed in his room, and unlike Martha she enjoyed it very much.

She woke around midnight and made her way back to her own room. There she listened to sporadic gunfire coming from a nearby street. Somebody ran by shouting on the sidewalk below and she heard two more gunshots and a scream, and then sirens. She thought of Martha and David and what she had seen and done in the last two months, and she thought of the same French who had built Chartres and made fashionable clothes out of rags. Eros and Thanatos stalked not only the fields of war by day and night, but also the cities and towns and the fields of light.

EISENHOWER, THE RUMORS NOW SAID, HAD NEVER INTENDED TO liberate Paris. His plan all along had been to skirt the capital and avoid the destruction of monuments and the interminable house-to-house fighting that would inevitably follow. It had been de Gaulle's unceasing political pressure that led him to change strategy and march into the City of Light. But he had no idea of resting there. North of Paris the war went on, and at the end of the month the lipstick-covered GIs began to stream out of the city toward the battlefields. A day after their dinner, David Schuyler packed his own photographic gear, gave her a cheery buss, and set off with the Third Army toward Brussels.

Annie was not yet ready to leave. *Vogue* wanted more photographs of the liberated city. Before he left, David suggested she send some of her pictures, free-lance, to the editors at *Life*, and she spent two more days at the Scribe, working on a story to go with the photographs. Meanwhile, rumor had another Allied offensive taking shape in the Netherlands—the greatest airborne attack in history, it was said, "Operation Market Garden," the brainchild of the widely despised, beret-wearing, cocksure British martinet Field Marshall Bernard Montgomery, who had promised Eisenhower that, if let off his leash, he would end the war before Christmas.

Annie cared about soldiers, not strategy. She filed story after story about the wounded boys in the hospitals, the battle-weary American boys suddenly let off their own leashes in the most sensual city in the world. She had no idea whether *Vogue* wanted these sketches. Martha-like, she simply kept writing.

And of course, the Muse of Coincidence was looking down with her usual bemused expression. On the morning of September 9, as she passed through the luggage-cluttered lobby of the Scribe, Martha herself, wearing a huge smile and a glamorous sash of white bandage across her torso, stepped out of the cable room. Persuasive and cajoling as ever, she somehow got them into the bar, in theory closed until noon, and seated at a table with a bottle of Red Label scotch and two nearly clean glasses.

She had been in Italy again, yes, and had gotten around all military restrictions to stay as close as possible to the fighting men. During the battle for Florence she had been billeted in a house with an elderly expat American woman. The apartment looked out over a garden toward Fiesole. A British artillery unit had set up shop in the garden, but the British captain in charge of it liked to sneak inside to play the piano while the American lady sang Italian love songs and, as Martha later wrote for *Collier's*, "outgoing shells from our artillery whistled over the house like insane freight cars."

Over a second bottle of scotch that night, Martha showed her some pages she had just cabled off, describing her wild ride from Florence to the Adriatic coast—"Italy was a jigsaw puzzle of fighting men, bewildered terrified civilians, noise, smells, pain, fear, unfinished jokes and high explosives." Flak in the sky had looked like exploding tennis balls. She had watched a pilot drop from a burning plane and parachute down out of a brilliant blue Mediterranean sky, dangling in the air "like Icarus on fire." (Annie sighed and thought of her own plodding, earth-bound prose.)

The bandage, she explained, covered a broken rib, achieved when the jeep she was riding in hit a ditch in the dark and rolled over twice. She grinned wickedly. "I wrote Ike to ask for a Purple Heart."

While they ate at the Hôtel Lincoln—Martha, always resourceful, had found a nicer, cheaper room there—a bottle-blonde AP reporter stopped by their table.

"Hemingway," she purred at Martha, "is stopping at the Ritz. I thought you'd be there with him, dear."

Martha's eyes went dead.

"He has a room down the hall from Mary Welsh," the reporter added. "He calls her 'Small Friend.'"

"A darling person," Martha said.

The blonde shrugged and left. "My rib hurts," Martha said and ended the meal early to go up to her room.

THE NEXT MORNING THE ARMY PRESS OFFICE ARRANGED A TRIP for journalists to newly discovered Gestapo torture chambers on the avenue Foch and at a suburban town called Chatou. They were the only women in the group. While Martha scribbled notes that she would later metamorphose into a prize-winning article on the "wounds" of Paris, Annie tried to capture on film the wet tunnels and windowless cells beneath the street, many of the floors still an inch deep in water. Prisoners had been held here until they were carried upstairs to soundproof chambers. Or else they had been simply left to starve. At Chatou they saw a wooden shack in a garden. Its interior walls were stained brown with dried blood. A prisoner had somehow scratched on a wall, "*Vengez-moi.*" Avenge me.

"I wonder," Martha said, "if it was a man or a woman."

That night, as Annie packed to leave for Brussels, Martha came by her room with an invitation. There was an officers' party that night at the Prince de Galles Hôtel, and though Martha ordinarily avoided the non-fighting officers she called "the braided set," some of her old pre-war friends would be there and she hated to miss a good party.

Annie looked at her battered rucksack on the bed, her steel pot helmet, the army boots that would replace her leather flats tomorrow, and allowed herself to be led downstairs to somebody's waiting Buick.

At the Prince de Galles' porte cochère a footman ushered them into the once elegant lobby, now mostly denuded of furniture and clients but brightened by the French passion for cut flowers, which overflowed a rank of vases by the reception desk. Upstairs at the ballroom door, Annie stopped on the threshold, peering in at a milling crowd of crisply dressed American and British officers and carefully made-up young French women—"Their nieces," Martha muttered caustically. Annie hesitated until Martha, who had sailed confidently ahead, turned and motioned her forward.

And in the second of the four moments that would destroy her moral universe, she heard Martha say, "Come and meet the Twins!"

# Six

THE TWINS DIDN'T RESEMBLE EACH OTHER IN THE LEAST.

Shaw, the one on the right, stood about five feet nine. He was wiry and pale, and his eyes had a startling blue intensity that, she would find out later, could turn suddenly cold and flat, like disks of ice.

The other one was B.T. (for Bennett Templeton) Adams and he looked like a skinny, Yankee version of Prince Valiant in the comic strip—just over six feet tall, with wavy, straw-colored blond hair that somehow the army had not clipped down to standard fuzz. He had a long, deeply lined face, quietly handsome, and incongruously big hands that might have belonged to a stonemason or a concert pianist. They were both twenty-six years old.

Shaw was the killer. John Michael Shaw. On the right shoulder of his uniform jacket, under his captain's bars, he wore the Eagle's Head patch of the 101st Airborne Division and on his chest a Silver Star, two Bronze Stars, and a Combat Badge. Adams wore the same 101st patch and captain's bars, some battle ribbons, but no combat medals.

41

"We call them the Twins," Martha gaily explained, "because they were roommates at Harvard and they fight with each other all the time."

Shaw gave a wary, slightly cockeyed smile and nodded hello. Then a busty French "niece" tapped him on the shoulder and without a word he slipped away, rudely, Annie thought, toward the bar. Adams was protesting good-naturedly about the "Twins" nickname when Martha, in her element, surrounded by chattering people, bright lights, and drinks, simply took his arm and led him onto the dance floor. A five-man combo took their seats and the crowd began to pair off.

That left Annie standing by herself in the center of the room. It was the kind of party she was no good at. In college they had been called "jolly-ups" and consisted drearily of the cool, self-confident ones dancing in a gymnasium while the shy, self-conscious ones took to the walls, boys on the right, girls on the left. *Plus ça change*, she thought, and let the sentence die away.

She recognized a few faces from the Scribe, but really she knew nobody here, she shouldn't have come at all. She took off her glasses and wiped them on her sleeve. She felt just as thin and flat as she had felt at the horrible jolly-ups. She should have packed her kit and gone to Brussels with David, who was a serious person. A passing waiter gave her a glass of warm champagne and she edged backward toward the darkest part of the room and started to calculate how long it would take her to walk back to the Scribe because the Métro still wasn't running and finding a cab was a joke.

"I think I had your father at prep school," the killer Shaw said, stepping out of shadow.

Annie wheeled around.

"In American History," Shaw said. "He was a good teacher. An 'enthusiast,' but he didn't like that word."

Annie nodded and put her glass on a windowsill. Terrible champagne. Her father always said that "enthusiasm" came from Greek and meant a god was talking through you, which was nutty. In the eighteenth century it was an insult to call somebody enthusiastic.

"He was also, he liked to say, a 'devout Jeffersonian.'"

Annie nodded again. Thomas Jefferson and her mother were the only two of her father's infinite passions that had never wavered.

"He told us once he would willingly crawl up the hill to Monticello on his hands and knees, to honor Jefferson," Shaw said with his odd intensity, and Annie burst out laughing.

"Well, he took us to Monticello once, my mother and me, when I was about ten, but I'm pretty sure he stayed upright the whole time."

The band swung into an especially noisy rendition of the "G.I. Jive" and Shaw motioned her toward the door. On the dimly lit landing outside the ballroom a few couples were embracing near the curtains in what even her father would have called an enthusiastic manner.

"I must have seen you around the school," Shaw said. "All the teachers lived on the campus. And Martha said you were from Byfield."

"You wouldn't have noticed me," Annie said, "I was just a kid," and to her annoyance he agreed.

"Probably not." He took a swallow of champagne. "We move out day after tomorrow," he said, "so it's goodbye to Paris, I'm afraid. It's the only city I've ever liked. I hated Boston." He handed the glass to her. Like one of the cool kids, she took the glass, half drained it, and handed it back. "How is your father anyway?"

"He died last April. He had a stroke."

Shaw looked down at his glass. "I'm sorry." A long but not awkward pause. "*Requiescat in honore.*"

Annie didn't like people who quoted Latin. She didn't like to think about her father's stroke. "So, am I allowed to ask where you're going? It's the Code of the Journalist to ask."

He gave the same wary smile. "Well, I'm not headed to Monticello, anyway." Another pause. He looked tense and aggressive, but his manner was remarkably gentle. "I just wanted to say hello to Mister March's daughter. I might have ended up teaching history, like him. I did for a year or two, in fact, at Governor Drummond. I probably would have kept on that way, out of inertia. Except suddenly…." He turned one hand out in a gesture that meant war, Paris, the crippled world outside. "Suddenly, school was out."

One of the girls by the curtains moaned and the accelerating rustle of clothing grew unmistakable. Eros and Thanatos. Shaw took her elbow and led her down the stairs and into the lobby, where there was only a tired clerk at the reception desk, drinking what was probably Muckefuck, and a white-haired Frenchman in a dark suit, asleep in a chair. The doorman stared out the window. The "GI Jive" upstairs settled into a mutter.

Shaw walked around a table and sat down at an upright piano that had been shoved into an alcove. He ran his fingers through a few scales. "Out of tune," he said, "but not too much," and he began to play, slowly at first, then rapidly, confidently.

Annie knew next to nothing about music, but she realized with a blush that she wanted to impress him, so she cleared her throat and said, "Bach?"

"Mozart."

"Oh."

"Mozart said he wrote music the way a cow pisses," Shaw said with a grin, and while she was still laughing he banged the piano closed and swung around on the bench. "I thought I'd take a little Thomas Jefferson tour of Paris tomorrow, starting with the house he had on the Champs-Élysées."

An expectant pause. When he grinned, he absolutely did not look like a killer. "I'd love to go," Annie said, with another blush.

# Seven

THOMAS JEFFERSON, AGE FORTY-ONE, NEWLY WIDOWED, CAME TO Paris in the summer of 1784 as American Minister Plenipotentiary to France. He had never been to Europe. He spoke French, but he had learned it from an itinerant Scot in Virginia, so bizarrely enough he spoke it with a thick Scottish accent. France changed him, of course, Shaw said, the way it still changes most Americans—he met royalty, he witnessed the bloody start of the French Revolution, he learned how to make ice cream, and he had a passionate love affair with one Maria Cosway, an Englishwoman whose husband was a disreputable painter.

"How come disreputable?" Annie said.

"Evidently he painted pornographic snuff box lids," Shaw said, and Annie guffawed so loudly that Shaw gave another of his cockeyed grins.

"Not that your father ever told us. I found that out on my own."

"I refuse to think about it," Annie said and turned to make a waving gesture toward the street. "So there was a toll gate right here?"

"Here" was the Champs-Élysées, where they were standing in front of a non-descript building in which, according to a plaque on the wall, Thomas Jefferson had lived from 1785 to 1788. Rain was falling in a half-hearted, indecisive way, and she was shivering under an umbrella liberated from the Hôtel Scribe while Shaw, in green and brown fatigues today, stood bareheaded on the sidewalk, squinting at the plaque. Behind them, two American tanks clanked and rumbled down the famous avenue.

This was the third stop on their tour. They had begun with the Palais-Royale, where the great Jefferson had dined and joined a chess club, then gone on to the rue Taitbout where he had briefly lived (no plaque), and now Shaw launched into a charmingly earnest lecture about the toll gates of the *Ancien Regime* and the Revolution, and Jefferson's friend, the hopelessly naïve General Lafayette.

Annie listened with half an ear. She had no idea what to make of Shaw—he was funny, comical even, just enough older, bursting with oddball information like her father. But once in a while, when their jeep rolled past a wrecked American tank not yet cleared from the street, for instance, his face had frozen, his jokes had stopped. Instinctively, she had glanced at his chest where yesterday he had worn the medal Martha called "the Silver Star for Slaughter."

Worse, so far, he had been a perfect gentleman.

AT THE JARDIN DU LUXEMBOURG, THEY STROLLED THROUGH THE soggy gardens—blessedly free of Jefferson associations—and then, with the rain chattering on the canvas top, they sat in the jeep he had somehow gotten from the motor pool and ate *sandwiches jambon* and drank red wine from a bottle. Inevitably, Shaw asked how a nice girl like her had ended up wearing army boots and an Eisenhower jacket, in the bloodiest place in the world.

When she was younger, Annie loved to talk about herself, she had loved to fill out applications and questionnaires that listed her schools, her honors degree in French at Radcliffe, her incredibly boring year teaching at the Shady Hill School, her next two years at the *Springfield Republican*. None of it seemed important now. So she remembered her mother's saying—"Most men confuse conversation with autobiography"—and asked Shaw about Harvard.

"I read classics," he said.

"Did you kill a lot of Germans?" A French boy about twelve or thirteen leaned in the jeep on Annie's side and grinned at Shaw. His English was perfect, his face was flushed, and the beret he wore was soaked black from the rain. "Did you kill them all?"

"All I could, kid."

The boy looked at Annie. Like most Parisian children he was extraordinarily thin, as if his bones had been plucked bare by the war.

"I saw his badge, 'Screaming Eagles 101st,'" the boy said. "They're the best. Paratroopers. I live over there." He pointed to an apartment building where every other window was boarded up. Even from fifty yards away Annie saw big spidery pockmarks and smaller bullet holes running up and down the walls, and part of her wondered how she had come to know the difference between bullet holes and artillery shells. "They raped my sister," the boy added, and she felt her stomach turn. She thought he was about to cry.

"Got no chocolate, kid, sorry," Shaw said roughly.

The boy ignored this. "I walked to school across the Jardin," he said, "every morning, and the Bosches had their tanks lined up by the *ruches d'abeilles,* and they used to shout stuff at us. My friend Henri did the goosestep in front of them once, just to be funny, and they broke his leg with a crowbar." He leaned in farther, face hard and red, and Annie saw that he was not going to cry, not ever. "Kill them fucking all," he hissed.

They rode back to the Scribe in silence. When Shaw pulled up behind an army bus and twisted toward her on his seat, she thought he was going to kiss her and she suddenly thought this was not a good time, not the right time at all. He read her mind, of course.

"At college," he said, "I wrote my thesis on Cicero and 'the Just War.'"

"Not Thomas Jefferson?"

Shaw shook his head with the same wary grin that she was beginning to recognize as infinitely sad. "Jefferson was a noncombatant." He pushed the gearshift lever and put in the clutch. "See you in Berlin," he said.

THAT NIGHT SHE MET MARTHA AND B.T. ADAMS IN THE BAR OF the Scribe, which was now, by comparison with two weeks ago, practically deserted.

"All moved out," Martha said, frowning at the mostly empty room. She was, as she had told Annie when she sat down, two scotches away from being drunk. She exhaled a little V of cigarette smoke from her nostrils, a trick she had only recently taken up, and made the dismissive wave again. "Every little body gone. Gone north. *Moi aussi,* day after tomorrow. You too, my mouse, if you want to come with me."

"I've hitched a ride in the morning to Lille," Annie said, "in a six-wheeled truck. Just me and a couple of armored divisions."

"Don't look now," B. T. Adams said.

Martha looked. "Oh, *her.*" She twisted back in her chair and lit a new cigarette off the old one. "It's 'Small Friend,'" she told Annie. She blew smoke in the direction of a curly-haired brunette taking a seat twenty feet away at the bar. "'The Huntress Mary Welsh,' looking for prey. But *he's* not here, thank God."

Adams looked at his wristwatch with a brisk thrust of his sleeve. "I need to take you back to your hotel, Martha. We're moving out tomorrow."

"Somebody here will give me a ride."

"I don't suppose you can tell me where you're going?" Annie said.

"He's going to Holland," Martha said. "The whole 101st is going to Holland and then east through the Ardennes. Christmas in Berlin."

Adams sighed. "Martha, you should really be locked up and muzzled."

"Are you going with Captain Shaw?" Annie asked.

Adams took a cigarette from Martha's pack and tapped it against his left wrist, the way men do. "You know," he said, "sometimes I think Shaw is just going to disappear in a puff of smoke and rematerialize as a character in a Russian novel," which Annie saw was no answer at all to her question.

He stood up and looked down at them. He was quite tall and quite handsome in a preppy kind of way. "I'll look for your photographs, Miss Annie."

"You'll have to subscribe to *Vogue*."

He laughed, bent to kiss Martha and left.

"I knew his family in St. Louis," Martha said. "Poor as church mice. He was a scholarship boy at Harvard." She looked at her glass and seemed annoyed and surprised that it was empty. "I'm going to go get another drink and the hell with Small Friend. And yes, to answer your question, the beautiful Twins are in the same outfit and moving on to Eindhoven tomorrow, only Shaw is in a combat command and B.T. is in G-2 Intelligence."

There was a burst of laughter from the bar. Martha stood unsteadily and brushed her skirt straight with both hands. She started toward the bar, only to look back over her shoulder, owl-eyed like Athena. "I think he likes you," she said, and lurched away.

Which one? Annie thought.

# PART TWO

## Market Garden and the Netherlands
## September 1944

# One

"FUCKING *MUD!*" SHAW SCREAMED, BUT NOBODY COULD HEAR him because he was face down, plowing a line in the ground with his nose, and a hundred yards ahead of him the world was coming to an end.

"Fucking *Brits!*" he said because nobody had told them the field would be so mushy and wet. He lifted his head and started crawling toward the Apocalypse.

He had jumped on the far edge of the Drop Zone—an enormous grassy pasture now beginning to disappear under roiling clouds of smoke. He had jumped just where he was supposed to, but the flak was heavy and some of his troops were coming out late. He could see hundreds of parachutes, as if somebody had emptied a bucket of confetti in the sky, white specks drifting down from the circling C-47s, through the flak, through the black smoke, through the crump-thump pandemonium of propellers, mortars, 88s, Stens, and every machine gun in Europe letting go at once. It was like jumping from sunshine into midnight.

Off to the left one of his lieutenants was being violently ill in a ditch. Shaw scrambled to one knee and began to run toward the yellow flag that marked the regiment meet-up point.

As he churned through the mushy Dutch polder he saw that in the trees, the Zoenche Forest, where the Germans weren't supposed to be, anti-aircraft guns had found their aim and were turning the sky into a patchwork quilt of gray and black puffs of smoke. They must have started firing incendiary bullets, he thought, because now one after another the paratroopers were bursting into flames, human torches now, floating in the wind like sparks.

At the meet-up flag the men were straggling in, ducking and dodging over the open field until they reached the bulked-up shelter of a canal berm. Shaw let his sergeants herd them into order. He bent over like Groucho Marx and duck-walked along the berm until he met up with Major Samson Warrack, who wore a .45 in a holster like Patton and a pencil smudge mustache like Monty, and in a past life owned a chain of dry good stores in eastern Kansas. There was no past life anymore, of course. The past had caught fire and burned a long time ago.

Without a word Warrack handed Shaw his binoculars and pointed—bursting through the black smoke, droning and screeching as they dived, RAF Spitfires had arrived over the Drop Zone and they were methodically raking the forest ahead of them, left to right, blasting the trees to splinters. Shaw turned away and focused the binoculars. Above the smoky field he could see the C-47s and the gliders and the Spitfires still coming, hundreds and hundreds of them, a glittering silver line of planes, a sky train, that must have stretched all the way back to England.

Our Father who art in heaven—*stay right there!* Shaw prayed. *Down here is no place for You.*

He crouched and refocused and tried to find the bridge that was worth his life to capture.

OPERATION MARKET GARDEN WAS A LARGELY BRITISH OPERA-
tion. Its author, Field Marshall Bernard Law Montgomery, the
black beret-wearing hero of El-Alamein, intended that British
troops would have the glory of ending the war. Americans, as was
only right, would play a secondary role.

His astonishingly bold plan required the biggest airdrop in the
history of warfare in three distinct zones, from the Belgian border
to the ancient Dutch city of Arnhem some seventy miles north.
British forces were to circle Arnhem and secure the city's bridge
across the Lower Rhine, while American paratroops opened the
road farther south to yet more British units coming up from Belgium. Arnhem, once taken, Montgomery assured Eisenhower,
spelling it out with his usual condescension—once Arnhem was
taken by the British, the rest of the Allies could storm across the
river and into the Ruhr Valley—Berlin by Christmas!

But first there were the seventy or so miles of German-occu-
pied Dutch farmland to traverse.

Some mistakes in war can be forgiven. Both British and
American intelligence believed that the Germans in Holland were
few in number, poorly armed, and in a state of panic. In the confusion of planning, nobody paid much attention to the German
Fifteenth Army, which was bottled up and trapped in the Scheldt
Estuary, miles west of the drop zones, under siege by the Cana-
dian First Army. That was the forgivable mistake.

The unforgivable mistake was ignoring the map of the
Netherlands.

The road from Belgium to Arnhem was a single lane highway,
much of it situated on top of dikes, and all of it crossing and
re-crossing bridges over canals and, at Nijmegen, the one hundred-yard wide Waal River. As the Dutch Resistance repeatedly
pointed out—and Monty repeatedly brushed aside—in rain or
in smoke or in fog, tanks and trucks could easily slip off the road

and slide into the canals. And in the event of mechanical break-downs, traffic on the narrow road could be blocked and stalled for miles. And in the event of German counterattacks, bridges up and down the corridor could be lost or blown apart, after which the highway to Arnhem could be sliced into pieces like a sausage on a plank.

The inexplicable mistake—for an Englishman—was forget-ting the weather. But that would come later.

"FUCKING *MUD!*" SOMEBODY SHOUTED IN THE SMOKE BE-hind Shaw.

Shaw would have laughed, but he was standing knee-deep himself in the same mud and slime as the trooper, in an irriga-tion ditch to the left of a one-lane dirt road that ran right past the southern edge of the Zoenche Forest. The forest stood like a brambly green island in the middle of the low, flat farmland, a mile or so across, a mile or so deep. It was the only obstacle between the Drop Zone and the town of Zon, where the north-south highway to Arnhem crossed over the Wilhelmina Canal. And it was supposed to be harmless and unimportant, because Monty's Intelligence had said there were no Germans in it.

No plan survives first contact with the enemy, that was the cliché.

Warrack motioned him forward and pulled out his clipboard. Warrack was the only man Shaw had ever seen who went to war with a clipboard. Lying on his belly, ticking off points with a pencil stub as calmly as if he were writing up inventory in one of his dry goods stores, he sketched the ditch they were hiding in, the forest, the bridge at Zon. The plan had been to march around the forest and through the town to the bridge. But marching that way in the open fields, now that the Germans had brought up artillery, would be suicide.

"So you're gonna take a walk in the woods," Warrack said.

"Look at that." The company medic had just slithered up to them and all three turned to watch a paratrooper falling from the sky. Somehow he had slipped out of his harness in mid-air and now he was plummeting earthward like a stone. He hit the fuselage of a landed glider, then the ground. Even through the din of guns and planes, Shaw heard the whump of impact. The trooper's arms and legs flung out, they heard the bones crack and watched him grow smaller and smaller as he rolled like a ball across the turf.

"No point going after that one," the medic said.

Company D, First Battalion of the 507th consisted of three platoons, 150 men, Shaw's men. Shaw didn't mind that they also called him "Captain Harvard" behind his back because they were his men and they said it with a mixture of amusement and awe. No other officer, they told the other companies, carried little volumes of Latin into combat. Nobody else killed with such intensity, nobody else took care of his people so tenderly.

Overhead the gliders were still coming down by the dozens, but the Spitfires had been called off and Company D was formed up, ready to fight. Shaw did his duck walk to the front of the ranks, then straightened and waved his arm and charged the forest.

Behind him the sergeants were shouting—"Hubba-hubba-one-time!"—and behind the sergeants the men were coming out of the ditch like men rising out of the ground.

They made it ten, twenty yards into the forest itself, when suddenly the trees exploded overhead—limbs, leaves, enormous splinters and smoke—bark, dirt, dust, red hot shell fragments flying in all directions. Shaw saw his favorite sergeant blown in half at the waist. The medic's right leg disappeared in a pink mist. Somebody yelled "Booby traps," but there were no booby traps, just machine guns and the pump-screech-concussive blasts of German 88s, firing from the other side of the woods.

Methodically, furiously, to the sublimely insane chant of "Hubba-hubba-one-time!" Company D went about the business of advancing through the disintegrating trees and brush. The four platoons spread out in a two hundred-yard line, Lieutenant Sizemore on his left, Wilcox and Aikens on his right. Sometimes in the smoke Shaw lost sight of everybody but Wilcox. Sometimes he saw the German helmets he was shooting at. Sometimes his brain went haywire, unable to process the bedlam of noise, and for a blessed moment everything went eerily silent, everything moved in pantomime and slow motion, muted like a dream.

Major Warrack appeared on Shaw's left, where he shouldn't have been, waving his absurd clipboard. An 88 shell exploded above them and blew the sky open and a shell fragment sheared Warrack's face in two, vertically, as cleanly as a saber. Deaf again, Shaw felt himself blown sideways against a tree, then half buried under falling branches and leaves. When he rolled over on his back and looked up, half of Warrack's head was caught in the limbs above, staring down, one eye intact, the pencil smudge moustache gone, the clipboard gone.

Shaw struggled to his feet. On the left, at the edge of the woods, the bloodied remains of Lieutenant Sizemore's platoon were converging on the first of the two 88s. But the big gun in front of Wilcox's platoon stood some fifty yards beyond the woods, half a football field, out in the murderous open, where the book said you never ever charge without artillery.

"Hubba-hubba-*fuck*!" Shaw ran back and flung himself flat on the ground next to Wilcox. The 88 in front fired at treetop level and an invisible fist seemed to punch the trees sideways.

"Gotta move back!" Wilcox yelled. "They're killing us!" More splinters and branches rained down. Wilcox was saying something else, but Shaw couldn't make it out. Wilcox was from Bemidji, Minnesota, long-necked, cheerful, unnaturally pale like every other Minnesotan Shaw had met, and a very good officer. A small, still sane part of Shaw's brain registered that now Wilcox's cheerful white face was streaked with red like an Apache and his bloody mouth was fixed in a wild grin, like a clown's rictus.

Shaw was not about to move back. Shaw was born to attack, his men said in wonder—when the *rage militaire* was on him, Captain Harvard turned into Geronimo. The "Fury" part of his brain, the part that had promised the boy in Paris to kill them all, picked a path to the 88 and pulled Wilcox up and started to charge, screaming like a madman.

Behind him, around him, the First Platoon rose and charged with him, into a whirling kaleidoscope of noise and smoke and flying colors, then sunlight, then green grass, then the white wall of sandbags stacked around the gun pit.

The 88 lowered, the gunners scrambled for a shell. Troopers swarmed over the sandbags. A German behind the gun took a bullet in the head and for an eternal second he was crowned by a halo of blood. The German at Shaw's feet dropped his hands and threw off his helmet, sobbing, crying. He was a boy, not more than sixteen or seventeen. He looked like a child playing soldier. *"Nein, nein. Nicht schiessen, bitte, nein!"*

Shaw aimed his rifle at the German's belly, then indecisive for once, or merciful, he lowered the gun to his side. The boy shot Wilcox in the throat.

IN THE AFTERMATH THEY FAILED TO CAPTURE THE BRIDGE. Company D had just pushed its way through a barbed wire gate and into the town of Zon—cheering Dutch citizens on every side, waving flags, blowing kisses—then they heard the crunch of dynamite and the bridge blew apart like an eggshell hit by a hammer.

# Two

WHAT MARTHA HAD SAID ABOUT THE TWINS—THAT THEY fought with each other all the time—was not really true. The fact was, despite their manifest differences, Shaw and Adams had been inseparable from the start and rarely fought. But then Martha told stories so well, she tended to impose them on people who puzzled her just for the drama of the thing, as most of her friends believed, or to put the world around her into better order, as Annie thought.

The Twins' coming together at all was the result of some quirk—or unexpected sense of humor—in the Harvard Dean's office, which assigned them to be roommates in E-31 of Eliot House, a notably preppy and affluent dormitory by the Charles River.

Shaw fit right in. He belonged to an illustrious old New England family—there had been Shaws in Boston since 1626, making (and keeping) a lordly amount of money—and his first name, Robert, was a tribute to a distinguished ancestor Robert Gould Shaw, who had led the first Negro regiment in the Civil War and whose statue stood prominently in Boston Common, just opposite the Harvard Club. Shaws had been going to Harvard since the seventeenth century.

Adams, on the other hand, arrived on scholarship from a public high school in St. Louis—Shaw went to Exeter—was the first in his family to go to college, and had no ancestors of any accomplishment. To supplement scholarship, he washed dishes in a Cambridge diner. He had been admitted to the College largely on the basis of his gifts in mathematics.

The physical differences were what you saw first, and perhaps saw with a certain bemusement. The blond Midwestern commoner Adams took to Harvard and its ways like a fish to water and quite rapidly transformed his accent, his wardrobe, and his general appearance, so that most people took him for the preppy and the shorter, darker, wirier Shaw, for the public-school man.

The intellectual differences were also great. Shaw read classics, not very diligently, and usually ended a semester with a report of two As and two Fs. Adams sailed effortlessly through Harvard's Mathematics Department and in his junior year began taking courses in the graduate school. When he enlisted in the army, he had completed all but one requirement for his Ph.D. It was this reversal of roles that most puzzled Martha.

The similarities were deeper. Both men had a firm—some thought rigid—sense of duty, not unlike that of Robert Gould Shaw. Each, in successive years, was president of the student charitable organization, Phillips Brooks House. Each devoted some hours each week to tutoring high school students in South Boston. Each had a sometimes crippling sensitivity to other people's pain, disguised in Adams's case by his slightly dandyish pose and in Shaw's case by intensity of manner and, when it suited him, gruffness.

They enlisted together on the same day, February 6, 1941 and were sent to officer's training school at Camp Devens,

Massachusetts. There the Army, doubtless operating on the military principle that the place for a square peg is a round hole, assigned the mathematical Adams, not to Engineering as he had requested, but to Intelligence. On *his* branch application, Shaw had written "Infantry" in every blank.

The Army was right about Adams. For his graduate studies in Math, he had learned German and French, which put him on the fast track for European duty. And once in action he had shown a remarkable ability to analyze and sort out the complex and chaotic field reports of enemy troop strength and order of battle. Even more important, to everyone's surprise he became a gifted interrogator of German prisoners, stern and implacable like a German officer, but also alert to their fear, reassuring, and in every case quick to recognize what Harvard called "persiflage" and the Army called "bullshit".

Shaw had never handled a rifle in his life. But like Adams at Harvard, he took to army ways with perfect ease. It was as if the two antithetical institutions opened up parts of their characters that had lain in shadow up to now. Shaw, not quite of sniper quality, became nonetheless a near-expert killer with the clunky M-1 rifle. And the Exeter preppy showed a completely unexpected sense of identification with the ragtag group of soldiers he commanded, a motley assemblage of high school dropouts, Irish laborers, and farm boys, motivated by patriotism, molded into a cohesive and terrifying fighting unit by "Captain Harvard." In his officers and noncoms he looked for these same qualities of empathy and fury. He had personally chosen Wilcox. Adams was strategy, Shaw liked to say. He was tactics.

AFTER THE BRIDGE AT ZON WAS DESTROYED, ARMY ENGINEERS were called in to rebuild it, but they made no progress at all, stopped cold again and again by German counterattacks. Until a new bridge was in place, the only way across the canal was a wooden footpath half a mile to the west, hardly the place to move a regiment of troops.

Meanwhile, as the engineers worked, the rest of the 101st moved south toward the market city of Eindhoven, the second of its assigned targets. On September 18, late in the afternoon, B.T. Adams turned up at regimental headquarters to confer with General Taylor's staff. And after he had made his report, like a needle swiveling on a compass, he found his way to Shaw.

Who was easy enough to find.

Company D had been placed in reserve for the moment and sent to quarters in a Dutch high school on the outskirts of town while the attack on Eindhoven went on. And Shaw was alone for once, taking a break in an empty classroom.

"The theory of paratroopers is simple," Adams said by way of greeting. He sat down heavily on a desk. "They're not infantry."

"You're so fucking pedantic," Shaw said. The outside wall of the classroom had been partially blown away, so that they had a panoramic view of formerly bucolic farmland now being chewed apart by smoke belching tanks and half-tracks, advancing toward Eindhoven. Everything in sight seemed to be on fire, haystacks, houses, even the grass, even the dirt. Ghoulish soot-blackened foot soldiers picked their way between flame pits while what they could see of the sky boomed and flashed and rained clouds of sparks. Shaw's Puritan ancestors would have called it a scene of hellish pestilence or plague. The classically trained Shaw thought it looked like an invasion of barbarians.

"They're not *infantry*," Adams said. "*Infantry* gets continuous support. *Airborne* fights three, four days, then you pull them out. You don't drop them behind the lines and forget them. That little weasel-face Monty has forgotten his people. He's using them like infantry and he's killing them."

"Nobody's forgotten anybody." Shaw was too exhausted to talk about incompetent generals. He had propped a broken mirror on an overturned table and now he began shaving himself out of his helmet.

"The First Airborne dropped at Arnhem," Adams said. "Nobody's talked to them since. Why? Because the idiot British gave them "22" radios and those things have a *two mile* range on a good day. And they were set in England to two *different* frequencies, so nobody can talk to anybody else!"

Artillery drowned him out for a minute.

"And one of the frequencies is the fucking *Dutch National Radio!* They're killing us." He stood up and pinched the bridge of his nose, as if to clear a headache. "Fucking Monty."

Shaw swished his razor in the helmet's cold water and squinted at the glass. "You know, I never did see a mirror that could do me justice."

Adams hesitated a beat, then laughed out loud.

"Old Charlie McCarthy joke," Shaw said, and, tension cracked, they both laughed at some pre-pestilence memory of the radio comedian. Somewhere close by a Sherman tank began to pump out rounds from its 75 mm gun, shaking the walls and showering them with falling plaster.

From the hallway another Infantry captain peered in.

"Too bad about Wilcox," he said sarcastically to Shaw.

Shaw stopped laughing and, as Adams later remembered it, his face simply froze. Granite could not have been harder or colder.

"You write the parents yet? Tell them it was your fucking fault he bought it, *Harvard?*"

Shaw turned slowly and stared at the captain.

"Pussy," the captain said and walked away.

Adams started to ask who Wilcox was, then stopped.

Outside, the tank fired one more round and clattered off. Shaw dropped the little mirror to the floor and carefully ground it to pieces with his heel.

# Three

On September 19, the third day of Operation Market Garden, the 101st made another attempt to get across the Wilhelmina Canal. This time a small tactical unit from Shaw's regiment set out to capture a secondary bridge at a village called Best, ten miles up the canal, west of Zon.

But (see Mistake Number One), no one had given any thought to the German 15th Army, believed to be still trapped far away on a peninsula near the Dutch coastal town of Flushing.

It wasn't. Somehow during the synchronized chaos of the first day of Allied landings, the 15th German Army had crept away unobserved from Flushing and made its way as far as the same village of Best, where it was now waiting, murderously poised to annihilate the small Allied force. Whereupon General Taylor did what B. T. Adams thought great leaders always do. He sent more men to die. Whereupon the Germans did the same, and what had started out as a minor skirmish soon turned into a "shambles"—a word Adams had been taught at Harvard originally meant "a butcher's slaughterhouse."

In fact, as he stood over a table map showing Holland from the Belgian border to Arnhem, he thought there was a better image than "shambles" for what he saw. Best—no one was joking about the name—looked like a malignant black magnet, growing larger and larger by the hour as staffers drew dark waxy pencil lines toward it on the map. Each line represented another American unit sucked unexpectedly into the battle. Blood red lines represented the Germans. If it were a Rorschach test he would have called it, not a magnet, but a cancer.

Adams himself was far from the magnet's pull. His whole Military Intelligence Group was still in Eindhoven, in fact, where the 101st had set up its HQ in another school, a modern undamaged high school on the outskirts of the city. He had planned to look for Shaw again that night, until a second glance at the map told him that Shaw's Company D had already joined the spidery black lines moving north toward yet another bridge.

In other words, he thought, one Twin was headed, in the army's unbearably pompous phrase, toward harm's way, while the other sat safely miles away, behind brick walls. Adams had no idea how he felt about that. They were not really twins.

At seven o'clock he made his way in the twilight to the officers' mess tent, but he had no appetite and plopped down instead on the hood of a jeep and listened to the distant battle. Artillery had joined the infantry now and was painting the northern sky a howling, thunderous red and yellow, like a bad Turner canvas, he thought, come demonically to life. He sat with his arms folded, watching *Götterdämmerung*.

"Harm's way." His mind jumped about, as it did when he was under stress—if they were back at Harvard, he and Shaw would have sat around bullshitting all night about "harm's way," arguing like hopped-up sophomores—was it a poetic phrase? Or a biblical reference? What did "way" mean anyway—a road? A method? A winding path in the kingdom of the harmlessly personified Harm? What prize idiots they had been back then, in the harmless kingdom of Harvard.

Adams was a staff officer. He had no men to command, no men to worry over, no men to send into harm's way. He was attached to a roving unit called the IPW, "Interrogation of Prisoners of War," and his job was to analyze field reports and interview German prisoners. There were long lulls when he could leave his desk and simply walk around, looking, listening, like a reporter.

While he was thinking about Shaw, he admitted to himself, he was actually thinking about Annabella March.

The high school consisted of two long parallel corridors, a U shape on its side. The lower corridor had been left to the Dutch civilians, who were still trying to teach their classes, amazingly enough. The upper corridor was given over to military—map rooms, radio rooms, strategy rooms, sleeping quarters for officers, all the little movable fiefdom that traveled with a two-star general.

In the bustle and confusion, there was no sign or map to identify the Press Room, but on a door at the other end of the military corridor, somebody had pinned a black-and-white photograph of a reporter sitting serenely in a ditch with his typewriter on his knees while just behind him soldiers on their bellies were firing their rifles into a forest. Under the photograph a caption: *"Carry on, Alan Wood, the Olivetti is mightier than the sword!"*

"You want a beer, Captain?" a voice said behind him. A tubby young Brit with a handlebar moustache reached around and pushed open the door. "You want a beer, we're all out of beer. Gin we got."

Gin they had, and Coca-Cola and two cartons of Belgian chocolate spread along a table. A military sized coffee urn had been liberated, probably from the officers' mess, but that was being largely ignored in favor of a makeshift bar where a dozen or so men and two women were regaling each other with stories.

A hurricane lamp near the door was lit, but otherwise blackout curtains kept the room spookily dark. The walls buzzed and vibrated softly, to the rhythm of the distant artillery. Light from the lamp licked at the shadows. No one paid Adams any attention. By the coffee urn two khaki-clad backs were hunched dolphin-like over typewriters. Everybody else was standing around an American reporter named Cronkite—Adams had met him in Normandy—a Texan, telling a story about his glider crash and a mix-up of helmets. No Annabella March.

The tubby Brit handed Adams a mug of gin that smelled like paint thinner, and because the thumps of the artillery were growing louder, Adams leaned in close and asked about Annie. A shrug. Shrugs from everybody as he worked the room. Cronkite finished his story to general laughter—crawling out of the wrecked glider, he had picked up a captain's helmet by mistake and everybody saluted him when he made it into the open. The two women reporters stood up to leave, and Adams put down his drink and followed them out. Neither knew Annie. One of them, the dirty blonde, looked him up and down and smiled and asked where he was from.

"Eliot House," he said perversely, just to be difficult, and started back to the Map Room. When he looked over his shoulder they were still studying him and smiling. Next to Annie March in the Hôtel Scribe, he thought, they looked as drab as cabbages.

LATE THAT NIGHT HE WAS BACK ON IPW DUTY, IN A MUSTY room that must have been the teachers' lounge before the Germans came. At midnight he called in the fifteenth or twentieth prisoner of the day, yet another eighteen-year-old from the

German Fifteenth Army, captured at Best in a firefight. He was skinny, hungry, and terrified, his head was shaved bald, and he kept glancing nervously at the corporal off to the side of Adams's desk, typing up notes of the session. There was nothing to be learned from him. He came from the Ruhr, his father was a steelworker, Hitler was a savior—were they going to torture him before they shot him? He wanted to know, because all Americans were pigs, and the English were Jews.

Six more after him, exactly alike except for the hair. Some had straw blonde hair like Adams, some were shaved bald, all of them hated America, all of them started to cry.

The last one, however, was different, an officer, a Signal Corps major who had studied mathematics at the Karlsruhe Institute of Technology and who affected a casual *bonhomie* just this side of mockery. He crossed his legs, produced a cigarette and an ebony holder and waited for the corporal to hand him a lighter. He had been captured only because of his limp, he said—he slapped one thigh with a glove—and he wondered where Adams had learned his not-too-bad German.

Adams played along. "At Harvard."

"Then you're intelligent," the major said. "And you know I'm not going to tell you anything. I'm entirely loyal to the Führer and my men."

"Let's start with the Fifteen's present order of battle."

The major blew smoke toward the corporal. "Another Harvard man?"

"Fuck you," the corporal said.

"How many artillery companies with you?"

The major said something slowly and almost gaily and after a moment Adams recognized it as Boltzmann's equation for measuring entropy, irreversible disorder.

He was too tired to keep it up. Tomorrow would be plenty of time to come back to the mathematical major. As he was standing and gathering his papers, the major also stood politely and still with his slightly mocking smile said, "I won't tell you anything about my unit, Captain, but I will tell you something about yourself, one university man to another. I am very good at reading faces, very intuitive."

"I don't give a shit," Adams said.

"I'm your prisoner, for the moment," the major said. "But I have my men, my work. You, however,"—he pronounced the German slowly and seriously—"*du bist aber einsam.*"

The sergeant grabbed his arm and marched him out the door. Adams stood shuffling papers and translating what the major had said. I am your prisoner. *You, however, you are free but lonely.*

# Four

By September 22, Operation Market Garden had begun to come apart.

All along the stretch of highway between Arnhem and the Belgian border, the Germans were counterattacking in force, and the Allied troops, undersupplied, restricted by the crisscrossing Dutch canals to the single north-south highway, fought a revitalized and relentless enemy, now stronger than ever with the arrival of two new Panzer tank divisions.

But September 22 was the turning point not because of Panzers or canals. In their elaborate planning, the Allied staff had apparently forgotten the English weather (see Monty's Inexplicable Mistake). September 22 was the turning point because that morning—typical for late September in England—a wet, miserable, and impenetrable fog smothered the entire southern half of the island. All airborne operations were canceled. No planes could take off. No supplies or reinforcements could be dropped.

German Field Marshall Walter Model, a celebrated military butcher in Russia and later to be a convicted war criminal, studied his meteorologist's reports. Then he stood over his maps and smoked half a pack of American cigarettes. At nine o'clock in the morning he stabbed a finger onto the map at the little town of Veghel, where there was a cluster of four different bridges, one of them crossing a major canal. Take Veghel, he told his staff, and the so-called "Market Garden" would be cut in half. And without air support, he added, the northern arm at Arnhem would quickly shrivel and die.

As so often in his murderous career, he was right.

SHAW HAD NO IDEA OF THE DISCUSSIONS GOING ON AT EITHER headquarters. Strategy was for generals. Tactics were for captains. And on the afternoon of September 24 his tactical challenge was to move Company D into Veghel without catching the eye of the Panzers.

He was not doing well. For one thing, he was still thinking about Wilcox, thinking about the German boy, thinking about the shot he didn't take.

For another thing, Company D was assigned to go up the main street of Veghel, through the town square, and over Bridge Number Three, where they were to dig into defensive positions and hold them against the Panzers. But he didn't see any Germans yet, so how would he know where to dig in?

*Fucking Generals*, Shaw thought. Paratroops didn't hold defensive positions. Paratroops weren't infantry. (Score one for the pedantic Adams.) He watched Lieutenant Sizemore lead First Platoon up to the last building on the right before the town square and wondered what the fucking war had done to his fucking vocabulary. His vocabulary. You will think about *anything* to avoid thinking about getting shot, he told himself, and began to decline in his head the Greek noun *strategos*, "general." He had reached the genitive plural (*strategon*) when Sizemore took his people across the town square at a lope and signaled "All Clear" from the other side.

Shaw came out of his crouch and ran to the same building on the right. He peered around the corner at the bridge. First Platoon was to cover while Shaw led the rest of the company across the bridge, to the other side of the town. The bridge was clear. Behind him, over his shoulder, he saw a middle-aged Dutch man on his roof, unconcernedly hammering shingles, while three stories down two armies played war in the streets. A teenage girl rode past Sizemore on a bicycle with wooden wheels.

I want to be Dutch, he thought. As commander, he should have stayed back and let Second Platoon come around him and cross the bridge first, but he thought of his famous ancestor Robert Gould Shaw who had led his black soldiers from the front, not from behind, and he hand-signaled "Follow Me" and stepped into the clear.

Spread out, running silently, the eighty men behind him had gotten within fifty yards of the bridge when the first Tiger tank appeared and the whole world shrank to a point of light and a puff of smoke.

AFTERWARDS, SHAW REMEMBERED THE MINOR BATTLE OF VEGHEL only in a swirl of images, not in a coherent sequence.

He remembered reaching the bridge and watching the water in the canal start to boil as shell fragments fell into it, hissing. He remembered watching the boiling water slowly turn red.

His incomparable soldiers had withdrawn on their own, back to the buildings around the town square. In the same buildings, in a dank, shaking basement that he was crossing to get to an alley, he saw his wounded people sprawled on the floor and dying. Some of them had been hit by phosphorous-tipped shells and glowed like ghosts in the dark.

Along the edge of the canal the gunfire from both sides became so thick that he thought he could reach up with both hands and grab bullets like honeybees or flies.

In the kitchen of a Dutch house, leaning against a wall and reloading his rifle, he heard musical notes from the next room, badly played because a machine gun was firing through the window and into a piano. Then, as his head swam, he heard someone typing and that was a typewriter upstairs, being chewed by bullets. Outside, the gold hands on a steeple clock were spinning crazily, hit repeatedly by stray bullets.

At some point Sizemore crawled up to him and said, "Captain, I don't think I'm dead. I'm talking."

One funny moment: on the other side of the canal the Germans were dug in. A scrawny Mexican kid named (he thought) Lopez, was out of grenades, so he picked up an apple, pretended to pull the fuse, wound up and threw it into a German foxhole, and while the terrified Germans scrambled to get out he shot them down, playing his submachine gun on them like a hose.

Another one: pulled back to the safety of a canal embankment, two of his people stood side by side shooting and singing an old Sunday school song: "In my heart there rings a melody of love, a melody of love, love, love."

Toward the end, they stacked dead soldiers and civilians in the streets like logs, four or five bodies high, ghoulish roadblocks. Lopez shot a German scout dog and began to cry. During a half-hour cease fire, cars and jeeps from both sides crossed the bridge to gather wounded and carry them back. As Shaw watched from a house overlooking the plaza, an SS trooper stopped a Red Cross jeep with four wounded GIs lying across its seats. He said something to the driver, then lifted a flamethrower and turned it full blast on the jeep.

# Pont Neuf

That night, mildly concussed by a flying brick, Shaw rested against the side of a tank and watched as a detail from First Platoon marched half a dozen German prisoners past him. Two minutes later he heard gunfire. The detail marched back, empty-handed.

"If you don't see it, Captain," Sizemore said with questionable grammar and a face like a block of wood, "it didn't happen."

"*Inter arma silent leges,*" Shaw said under his breath, and hated himself for being pompous. He hated himself anyway. He missed Adams.

He thought a good officer would have shot the German a hundred times before he let him kill Wilcox.

# Five

A *BRIDGE ALWAYS CONNECTS TWO WORLDS.* FROWNING, TONGUE between her teeth, Annie March read what she had just typed and then looked up to see the handsome face of Captain B.T. Adams reading over her shoulder.

"Where's your camera, mademoiselle?"

Annie flushed and stood up and took off her glasses.

"Here I thought you were *Vogue*'s ace photographer," Adams said, "but nary a camera in sight."

Annie ran a hand through her hair. "I just got here today, and I left it in my crib." She made a wry, self-conscious grimace. She had lately taken to using military slang, and she was finding she didn't really like it. A "crib" was your bunk or quarters, and it sounded stupid.

"I've been here three weeks. Do you mind?" Adams pulled the sheet of paper out of the typewriter and started to read.

Just like a man. Just like a *Harvard* man. Of course she minded. Of course she hoped that he would read it and put it down and say it was staggeringly brilliant, which was all any writer ever wanted. "Have at it, monsieur." She made a little pained moue and stepped back to give him light.

He needed light because it was ten o'clock at night and the room where she had installed herself to be alone was mostly shadow. Outside the blackout curtain she could hear rain. Rain was general all over Holland, she thought inconsequentially. A slow, sad rain, like the rain in Paris. The electricity in Eindhoven had cut off again, so for light she was using a battered old hurricane lamp she had found by the door.

"This was the Press Room when we first got here." Adams handed her the sheet of paper without comment.

"Well, sure," Annie said. "It still smells like a distillery."

Adams smiled the preppy smile that had been so charming back in the Hôtel Scribe, and he said, "Can a gent buy the newcomer lady a drink? They have a bar in the Officers' Mess."

"Coffee," she said. "I still have to finish this piece."

"Well, I think it's brilliant. I don't see what else there is to do to it."

"In that case," she said, and picked up the little typewriter. "Gin."

Operation Market Garden had officially ended on September 25, when the few surviving British troops at Arnhem slipped away from the Germans and retreated helter-skelter along the narrow corridor that led back to Veghel and Eindhoven. Then Veghel, too, fell back into German hands, and by the first week in October all of the Netherlands north of the Waal River was once more under German occupation.

Shockingly, Allied losses during the eight days of the operation had been greater than all the Allied losses combined on D-Day in Normandy four months earlier. Dead and wounded in Holland, British and American, amounted to something over 17,000 men. No one had yet counted up civilian deaths. Monty had never come to the battlefield command posts, because he was back in Brussels having his portrait painted. To the newspapers he proclaimed Market Garden a famous victory.

"It looks like you're here to stay," Annie March said. The electricity had come back on, and with it the lights in the Officers Mess. She took in the giant coffee urns, the two upright stainless steel freezers, and the bright blue 101st Airborne banner hanging across one wall of what had formerly been the high school's faculty cafeteria. "And dear God, what's in this drink?"

"That's a military secret," Adams replied, also looking around the room. Three or four other officers at a table. An orderly in a white jacket. Two British majors by the window. The Brits nodded in approval at Adams and his girl and grinned like a pair of alligators.

"Creosote is what's in it," Annie said and took a big swallow anyway. "Do you know where Captain Shaw is?"

"Why 'two worlds?'" Adams asked. "You said a bridge always connects two worlds."

Annie shook her head. "I was trying for something profound, something poetic and Martha-ish, maybe. I was looking across the river and imagining that on the other side, in Germany, the fields were neat and trim, the houses were intact, not ruins like over here, as if it were a different world. *Mysterious*, you know. *Hopeful*."

Adams looked down at his glass and hoped he wasn't being pedantic, as usual. Shaw would have told him to zip his lip. "Actually, that's still Holland over there. Germany is another few miles beyond the river and I'm pretty sure that part of it is a mess too."

"Oh." Deflated, Annie swirled her drink in its glass. "Oh."

He found that he was suddenly speaking too quickly. "But it's a good image. I read somewhere that the Navajos say that children are born by walking over a bridge into this world, and when you die you walk across it the other way."

Annie said nothing for nearly a minute. Then: "I'm supposed to write a piece about civilian life in Dutch towns now, after all the fighting."

"I can show you that. I can show you around Eindhoven." Adams then had to stop and stand up as the British majors harrumphed over to their table. He shook hands and listened to strange seesawing sounds—they were from the north of England and cheerfully incomprehensible. Shaw used to say that British English sounded like a woodchuck gnawing a sausage. When he sat back down Annie had a faraway look, as if she were rewriting her article and the rest of the world had vanished. Shaw used to have that same look.

"That's a Hermes typewriter you have there," Adams said. "I once wrote a paper in college about how typewriters changed literature." Annie murmured something as incomprehensible as British. "Mark Twain had a typewriter," he said, but he knew he had lost her. Five minutes later they said goodnight in the corridor, and he watched her walk purposefully away, back toward the Press Room to start writing again.

Obsessive, he thought. Really pretty, really smart, he thought.

The next morning, she showed up at his office, scrubbed and smiling, and asked him to give her a tour of Eindhoven.

Adams's Military Intelligence Company had been left behind when the 101st pulled back to Belgium, to interrogate POWs and deserters. But there were few of either these days. Meanwhile, his colonel had found a Dutch widow to occupy his time. His major was on leave. Adams was more or less his own boss. He signed out, closed his office, and led Annie to the city center to see her bridge again.

"I have no idea what it looked like here before," he said when they had tramped to an open plaza, a classic European civic space now surrounded by smashed, devastated buildings and inhabited by stray dogs and beggars. "But judging by what's left of the roofs and some of those carved doorways, this was probably the old part, the seventeenth century part. I know there was a small university campus down that road. But…" He shrugged. Eindhoven had been steadily bombarded for the better part of Market Garden, and most nights German artillery still fired harassing rounds into it at random. Every morning the Dutch pulled back their blackout curtains and came out of their houses and, like good burghers, swept broken glass from the streets.

Even beyond the city center almost no houses had survived the bombs and the shells. Annie took photographs of the ravaged plaza—the shell craters everywhere, the collapsed walls, abandoned battle trenches, ripped-up sidewalks littered with splinters and red brick dust and ashes. A bomb had gone off in a cemetery, literally raising the dead. Here and there the Dutch had piled broken glass into neat mounds. There was an unidentifiable stench and odd pockets of smoke in the air. Children played army with the innumerable brass shell casings strewn about by both invaders and defenders.

When he led her out to the fringes of town, they found a few markets and stores open and Adams helped Annie interview some women queued up to buy flour and ersatz coffee.

"The Germans *eat* paper," one of the women told them. "They *live* on it like fiends." And she showed Annie her thick book of ration slips, formerly issued by the German occupiers, now honored by the Allies, although there was very little food to sell and most women had ended up creating communal kitchens to feed whole blocks at a time.

"No heat," another woman told them. "We cook on wood fires." She snorted and waved one hand at the rubble around them. "Plenty of wood, though."

THE NEXT DAY HE BORROWED A JEEP AND TOOK HER FARTHER north to the town of Nijmegen—"Pronounce it any way you like," he said, and Annie laughed and wrote it in her notebook as a good lead sentence.

Nijmegen had a four-lane steel bridge across the hundred-yard-wide Waal River. They parked in the ruins of another city center plaza, the twin of the one at Eindhoven, and walked up to take a look.

"Two worlds here, for sure," Adams told her and explained that the shadowy horizon a few kilometers away was where the legendary Siegfried Line began, in German the "Westwall." Behind the trees and farm buildings lay a nearly impassable barrier of concrete bunkers and pits and the weird pyramidal Gothic structures called "Dragons' Teeth." Behind those, the mysterious Third Reich waited, crouched, poised on its stony thighs. A Messerschmitt reeled across the sky like an angry bird, and Annie shivered.

From the river they drove through the nearly silent city to yet another outlying schoolhouse, this one taken over by the local Dutch government to serve as a jail for collaborators.

It wasn't much of a jail. No bars or cells, just a series of foul-smelling rooms where arrested collaborators were guarded by a few uniformed policemen. In one room a nun sat by herself under a window. When Annie asked to take her picture she said nothing but sat up a little straighter. Another room held mothers and babies—the Dutch equivalent of French *horizontales,* though none of the women had shaved heads. The Dutch were kinder than the French. In another room they found old men playing checkers. Their crime was to have done business with the occupying Germans. In a kitchen two big farm girls, also collaborators—"soldiers' delights," Annie wrote in her notebook—were preparing the greasy soup and black bread sandwiches that would serve as the day's main meal. She closed the notebook and looked around at the bleak scene and said quietly, "Help."

*We've come to free them*, she thought, *and we've destroyed them.*

Afterwards, she took more pictures of the bridge and then, mood abruptly lightened, made Adams pose with a fishing pole while Dutch housewives chattered nearby, pointing and laughing. As turnabout, she showed Adams how to work the camera and struck a pose herself, hips cocked, glasses pushed up on her hair. One of the Dutch women took a picture of them both sitting on a bridge railing, arm in arm.

THAT NIGHT IN FRONT OF ANNIE'S CRIB, THEY STOOD AWKWARDLY for a long minute, studying the floor. Then Adams put one hand on Annie's cheek and kissed her. Slowly, methodically—he *is* a mathematician, she thought—he kissed her nose, her brow, and then her lips. He was sweet, affectionate, handsome. Annie thought of David Schuyler and how much she had liked it and how much she didn't want to be cold like Martha.

His hand found her breast and as she made the little gasping sound she always made, she thought how good it would be to have a warm, masculine body in bed next to her, with its strange, foreign planes and angles and hydraulic workings, a momentary stay against despair. She had been far from a prude in London and in Paris. Sex was what happened in a war. But she also thought— and she didn't know why, she had no idea why—maybe it was the women she had photographed in Chartres—she didn't want to do this.

Eros, Thanatos—she wanted something else. One of the girls in Paris said you make love *au feeling*. Adams was methodical but insistent. He put his hand on the point just inside her hip, where the electricity began. She brushed it away and he put it back.

Then, making herself clear, she pushed him away, not gently, and turned her back. Against her will she wondered what Shaw would have been like.

ON THE FOURTH DAY, AS ANNIE WAS PREPARING TO GO BACK TO Paris, Martha turned up in her patented pop-out-of-nowhere manner. "The turd that won't flush," Annie muttered to herself, oddly annoyed. And naturally, taking charge, Martha insisted that Annie stay another day and show her around Eindhoven.

Dutifully, Annie led her on a walking tour and then let her read the draft of her *Vogue* article, which Martha revised so well that Annie could hardly forgive her. At the end of the day she pleaded deadlines, changed her plans again, and caught a ride back to Brussels.

In the officers' mess that night the two British majors stopped by Adams's table and, with much good-natured sputtering and blowing, congratulated him on having, not one, but *two* different beautiful women at his beck and call, lucky chap. And by the way, where *was* the fetching little photographer?

"Ah," Martha said as they watched the majors harrumph and nod their way out of the room. "Like that, is it?" She shook a cigarette from a pack and called the orderly over to light it. "Though I suppose I would have guessed the other Twin."

"For God's sake, Martha."

She leaned forward and patted his hand. "But you're much handsomer, *mon vieux.*" She blew an expert smoke ring. "If not so rich."

"Oh come on, it was absolutely nothing. She's a nice girl, that's all."

He refilled his glass and drummed his fingers on the table. He cleared his throat. "Any advice?"

Martha laughed. "On affairs of the heart, I'm the last person to give advice. But I will tell you the one true thing I've learned over the years."

She paused so long that Adams resumed his drumming on the table.

"What I know," Martha said, "you fall in love the way you go bankrupt—gradually, then suddenly."

# PART THREE

## Paris
## November 1944

# One

UNLIKE MOST OF THE GREAT CITIES OF EUROPE, PARIS WAS STILL recognizable to anybody who had seen it before the war. It hadn't been bombed to rubble or twisted apart by artillery like London or Berlin—or Veghel or Nijmegen—its central monuments and buildings were still intact, its streets and stately avenues looked much the way they had since the middle of the nineteenth century. Even so, Shaw thought, it still had the air of a war zone.

In the thin, gray, mid-November light the buildings looked weary and drawn, old faces. Walls and doors were riddled with bullet holes from street fighting. All the windows of the great old Hôtel de Ville were boarded up. The occasional wrecked car or tank still sat along the fashionable avenues, not yet hauled away. A greasy film of gunpowder clung to everything. And of course, there was next to no electricity, so at dusk the streets went quickly dark, an ugly, coming-of-winter dark, and at night they became truly dangerous.

"Gangs," the doctor told him. "That's who's taken over the streets. Damn French spent the Occupation fighting Germans, now they're fighting each other—communists against monarchists, Gaullists against collaborators, black market boys, kangaroo courts, executions—I can't keep track of it. Some of the vigilantes, especially the communists, kidnap people in the middle of the night, just like the Germans, and then you never see them again. They call it '*épuration sauvage.*'"

"Wild purging," Shaw translated automatically.

"The brick hit you here." The doctor touched the back of Shaw's skull. "I can just make out the bruise. But you're not even tender now where it hit you. I've done every test in the book. You shouldn't be hurting in the back of your head at all. I don't know why your CO made you come see me."

"It doesn't hurt that much." Shaw looked at his watch. "I need to get back to Neuilly, sir."

"That's where your unit is?"

"We're refitting before we go back on the line."

The doctor was a lieutenant colonel, a rumpled, overweight white-haired Virginian, a neurosurgeon in real life, according to his diplomas. He had spent a considerable amount of time reading Shaw's folder and now he studied the Silver Star on Shaw's dress jacket. "You want to get back to your men?"

"Have to. Sir."

"Duty calls," the doctor said. He sat on the edge of his desk and opened the folder again. "And I bet you're always the first one to answer."

Shaw didn't like doctors. He wouldn't have come into Paris to the clinic if his major hadn't insisted. Thomas Jefferson said that when he saw vultures in the sky, he always looked around for the doctors. Ulysses Grant said when you didn't have anything to say, just don't talk.

"Who's Wilcox?"

This particular army clinic had been set up in a confiscated office building just across the street from the once fashionable Parc Monceau, north of the city center. Shaw sat on the examination table and carefully buttoned his jacket. Through the window the park looked autumnal and inviting, though to hear the colonel talk it was full of monarchists and vigilantes. He could hear ducks on a pond, communists probably.

"Wilcox was one of my lieutenants, sir. Killed last month."

The colonel closed the folder. "You want to talk about it?"

"No, sir."

The colonel sighed. "Pain likes to lie, Captain."

"That doesn't make sense. sir."

"Of course it does. Your concussion is healed. Your double vision is gone. You're doing OK. The pain you're having now is referred from somewhere else, the way pain usually is, but not somewhere physical is my guess—the word you want is 'psycho-somatic.' I think you should talk to somebody."

"I don't need a quack."

The colonel was already seated at his desk, opening the next folder. Without looking up he said, "That's a stupid thing to say, Captain."

"Yes, sir."

The colonel tapped the folder hard. "You came through Normandy on D-Day plus one and then through that farce up in Holland. You must have lost plenty of men before this Lieutenant Wilcox. Dead soldiers go with this business." He looked away, through the window toward the park, and he might have been talking about Shaw, or he might have been talking about somebody else. "Mistakes go with this business."

When you don't have anything to say, just don't talk.

"What I think," the colonel said to the window, "I think for you it was maybe just one dead soldier too many."

When you don't have anything to say.

The colonel rubbed his face with one hand, a weary, dismissive gesture. "This is Paris, son. Go find a girl."

SOME TWENTY KILOMETERS TO THE SOUTHWEST OF PARIS, THE other Twin was also staring out a window, and admitting to himself that, the hell with clichéd historical pieties, he really, really disliked the world-famous Château de Versailles.

B.T. Adams swiveled his chair away from his view of the garden and studied the gold fleur-de-lys on the wallpaper (cerulean blue). What historical obtuseness, he wondered, had led Eisenhower's staff to set up their headquarters in Versailles of all places—*Versailles*, the vastly absurd and absurdly vast palace of France's despotic seventeenth-century monarchs. Versailles was a symbol of *absolute royal power*, the very opposite of the great Allied democracy Eisenhower represented. Didn't these people read?

Shaw, the Jeffersonian, would hate it, Adams thought. He would hate everything about Versailles. He would hate everything about kings and courts. He would hate the pompous rigidity of the architecture and the self-conscious clipped and tortured symmetry of the garden. Whoever saw trees and flowers in nature like this? Adams swiveled back and frowned at the orderly rank of perfectly trimmed hedges under his window—square-shouldered, unnatural vegetation, khaki brown in the autumn chill, standing at attention like a company of brow-beaten soldiers.

Well, naturally, that was why the army had chosen Versailles.

He put his feet on his desk, just to create a little disorder. In its royal days, his little office had apparently been somebody-in-waiting's bedchamber. It was now minus the bed, of course, but still plus the fleur-de-lys, the gold ceiling molding, and an elegant glazed ceramic fireplace that his army predecessor had used as an ashtray. A sign outside the door pointed the way to the famous Hall of Mirrors, 357 twenty-foot-high mirrors, whose eye-popping illusions and multiplying reflections were a reminder that besides symbolizing absolute power, the labyrinthine palace was perfectly designed for evasion, intrigue, double-dealing. The army would like that too.

"You want the good news first, or the bad news?"

Adams stood up and grinned. "Always the bad, sir."

George Eberhardt came into the office and gave the throwaway salute that let you know he was one of the boys, but still a brigadier general, keep in mind.

"Bad news, I'm your new boss."

"That's horrible, sir."

"Good news, G-2 approved the promotion." He dropped a stout white envelope on Adams's desk. "Those are the oak leaves. You're a real live major now, detached to my shop for six weeks."

"Thank you, sir."

"OK, celebration over. Ten minutes to clear out of this pansy room and get over to my office. Can you find it? You won't get lost?"

Adams grinned again. "I'll order a car." Allied Headquarters took up about half of the Château, but bizarrely, the rest was still open to tourists, which in practice meant GIs on leave, who were notorious for getting lost in its endless maze of corridors. Early on, Patton had gotten lost and smashed down a door in frustration, only to find himself staring at a seventeenth-century brick wall.

"This is a very quick promotion, you know."

"Yes, sir."

"You're ambitious, I like that."

"Yes, sir."

"Ever think about the army after this is over?"

"I have, sir, actually."

"You do a good job in this, I can help."

Adams was not without some arrogance and some impatience. He wanted to say, "I always do a good fucking job, general," but he was also not without common sense and so held his tongue.

"Ten minutes," Eberhardt repeated, and ten minutes later to the dot Major Adams, pinning his new oak leaf insignias to his shoulders, walked into the general's second-floor office, where half a dozen staff officers, in impromptu conference, were studying a gigantic wall map of eastern Belgium. His was the lowest rank in the room, so the staffers ignored him.

"Desk." Eberhardt pointed over his shoulder at a spindly-legged antique table covered with folders, map cylinders, and stacks of what the general, a tax attorney before the war, liked to call "Interrogatories." Eberhardt was third in command of First Army Intelligence, and Eberhardt's "shop" analyzed maps and field reports and anything else they could learn about enemy troops in a sector running north and south the length of the eastern border of Belgium. What he had liked about Adams besides his ambition, he said, what made him pick out Adams from dozens of other junior intelligence officers, was first the quality of his POW interrogations, and second, his remarkable ability to turn abstract numbers into real places on a map, to think strategically. As a graduate of the lowly University of Arkansas, Eberhardt had added with undisguised pleasure, he also liked the idea of making a Harvard man his subordinate.

"So," Eberhardt said to the map, "Berlin by Christmas?"

One of the staffers snorted and tossed his head like a horse. "Berlin by Christmas" had been Monty's promise—and notorious five-dollar bet—to Eisenhower. But after Market Garden's collapse, that bet went politely unmentioned. After two months of horrendous fighting in the dense woods of what Belgians called the Hürtgen Forest, the Allies had pulled back, leaving the Forest they had fought so hard for lightly defended. Up and down the

German frontier, they were now policing their lines and waiting for spring.

"Here's what the Krauts are scared of." A cigar-chomping colonel stepped in front of Adams and thumped the map just below the southern Belgian border, where a quiverful of red arrows indicated the multiple armored divisions of Patton's Third Army, poised as if in mid-flight, sailing straight toward the Fatherland's belly. "Patton's going to move through right here and flatten them like pancakes."

"No. They've moved three more panzer divisions right in front of him, and the XIII SS just arrived *here,* from Russia.*"* This was another map-thumping colonel, contradicting the first. "They're not scared of Patton. That's bullshit. They're *waiting* for him."

"It's too cold," somebody said. "Even Patton doesn't want to fight the German winter."

As so often happened in conferences that touched on Patton's troops, this one deteriorated at once into a discussion of Patton himself, Patton's state of mind, Patton's mad-dog aggressiveness, how Patton had told *The New York Times* that he would go through the German lines like shit through a goose. Adams tuned them out. Adams thought that like football coaches and baseball managers, generals were wildly overrated. He walked closer to the map.

Many mathematicians are surprisingly tactile about numbers. Adams, for example, didn't think of them as abstract at all. He liked to touch them. He liked to say them out loud. He thought they had different textures, different skins, flavors. He had favorite numbers, he had other numbers (double primes) that he genuinely, irrationally disliked.

Now he drew one finger along the bristling concave line that stood for the newly arrived XIII SS tank division supposedly stationed just across the border from Luxembourg, waiting for Patton. But the contours of the map, the running numbers indicating changes of elevation, weren't any good for tanks. The numbers were too sharp-edged and jagged, the lines were too irregular, too hilly. If you turned the numbers into a real place, this wasn't tank country, this was Hall of Mirrors country. Adams moved his hands slowly, almost erotically, up and down the contour lines, caressing them. Lines from a risqué poem in freshman English popped into his head, a poet to his lover—"License my roving hands, and let them go/Before, behind, between, above, below"—and he thought of Annie March, and his hand stopped at a narrow gap in the mountains forty kilometers east of the Belgian town of Bastogne and he thought of Shaw.

Eberhardt was watching him closely. "You know your history, Major?"

"Not too well, sir."

"That's exactly where the Germans came through in the first War and again in 1940, just below the Hürtgen Forest, where all the fighting was in September. Now we own it, but your General Bradley in his wisdom has left exactly three infantry divisions there for defense, practically no armor. And the infantry are all replacements straight out of repple depple. They got zero for combat experience. Bradley says nobody's going to attack the Ardennes in winter conditions. But if I were Hitler, *I'd* attack it. Nobody expects it. He could split us right in half. Three lousy divisions to defend one hundred miles of front."

The cigar colonel shook his head. "Not gonna happen, sir. You're being a Cassandra, as usual."

Eberhardt muttered something unintelligible and turned away. Also from freshman English, Adams remembered that in the Greek myth, whenever Cassandra prophesied doom, the fun-loving gods made sure that nobody believed her. As part of the game, they also made sure that she was always right.

# Two

Go find a girl.

Go find Annie March.

At nine o'clock in the evening on November 19, Shaw walked into the bar of the Hôtel Lutetia and saw Martha Gellhorn at the far corner table, just where she'd promised she would be. And next to her, just as Martha had promised *she'd* be, Annie March turned toward him, hesitated. Smiled.

"I told you this is my new haunt." Martha waved him over with her cigarette. "Don't you think it's adorably tacky?"

She gestured expansively around the bar, which despite being in the heart of the Left Bank was decorated to look like a London gentleman's club—big leather armchairs, oak panels, squares of tartan on the walls, bad paintings of horses and horsemen and bewigged eighteenth-century ancestors of nobody in particular.

"This one." She pointed to a painting behind her. "What did Oscar Wilde say about fox hunting? 'The unspeakable in pursuit of the inedible?'"

Shaw slid into the seat next to Annie and searched for *le mot juste*. "Hello."

"Hello to you."

"I was just telling the ladies Hemingway stories." A slight, dapper man on Martha's left seemed to materialize out of the dark. This turned out to be a *Time* reporter named William Walton, whom Martha introduced as a master of diplomacy, since he managed to be friendly with her and also with another unspeakable she didn't care to talk about.

"Yes, you do," Walton said. "You talk about him all the time."

"Billy shuttles between us carrying messages about...*le divorce*." Martha signaled a waiter (who wore a kilt and a look of permanent embarrassment) and they shuffled glasses and bottles and ashtrays around to make room for Shaw's order. "Although once *you* start talking about him—" Martha was quite drunk, something Shaw had never seen before. Without pausing for breath she launched into a boozy account of Walton's exploits as a journalist—he was extremely brave, he had parachuted onto the beaches on D Day with the 82nd Airborne, the only newsman to jump. He wrote beautifully and fast, but such is perverse human nature he didn't care about that, he wanted to be a painter. He spoke French, German, Spanish, and for all she knew, Hungarian. He and Hemingway had spent a whole week together in August at Mont-Saint-Michel, drinking and arguing about religion.

"My husband is a Catholic," she told Annie. "Most people don't know that."

Serene and also drunk, Walton came to his feet and announced the need to "micturate."

"He is, bless his heart," Martha said as Walton staggered away, "a perfect beard." Annie frowned in puzzlement. "She doesn't know what that means, Captain Shaw," Martha said. "It means"—she leaned toward Annie and murmured with mock confidentiality, "it means he's the perfect escort. He's not interested in women."

"Martha, I need to get you back to the hotel." Annie began to search for her coat.

Martha sat back up. "When people say my husband is a 'man's man,' and you think about his spending a week with Billy Walton, it makes you wonder, does it not? However, from the way our Captain Shaw looks at you, my dear, I would say he is *not* a beard." She took a final swallow from her glass and stood up. "Although he *is* a Harvard boy. You never know. Take me home, dear girl."

"Don't go yet," Shaw said. "Please. I just got here."

"'Got' is the word that ate English. Kindly say, 'I have just arrived here,' not '*got* here.'" Martha had found her hat and coat and now she was gripping the edge of the table, swaying slightly. "I am," she said, "the ruins of my own castle, and Hemingway is the ghost that haunts it. Here comes Billy, all freshly micturated. Annie, I changed my mind. Billy can take me home. You stay here and console our soldier boy." She narrowed her eyes and bent over the table. "Do you read Chaucer, Captain?"

"Too modern for me."

"I quote Chaucer all the time. 'The woe that is in *marriage.*' 'The Wife of Bath's Tale.' Come on, Billy, the horse knows the way."

The Hôtel Lutetia was a huge Art Deco pile of Parisian limestone on the boulevard Raspail, opposite a little park and the Bon Marché department store. During the Occupation it had been used by German *Abwehr* counter-espionage units, which accounted, Shaw said, for the Nazi *affiches* and pennants you could see along the walls. They were mostly peeled away or torn to rags now, he admitted, but still visible in traces.

Outside, under an awning at the main entrance, they watched a slow, misty gray drizzle swing back and forth in front of them like a lazy curtain.

"There's a Métro station over there," Annie said, "but I'm not sure the trains are running."

"I don't mind the rain," Shaw said. "But my mother used to say I was so sweet I'd melt in it like sugar."

Annie laughed. "You're not *that* sweet."

Paris had been liberated for over three months, but because electricity was still rationed, only the big hotels and offices had reliable lights. They could see a few working streetlamps near the Métro station, but—like anti-moths, Shaw said—they turned right, away from the lights, and started to walk east, toward the shadowy warren of Left Bank streets that eventually led to the river.

"Where are we going?" Annie said. "Not that it matters. I hated that stupid bar. And I hated seeing Martha drink like that."

Shaw cleared his throat. "When I'm nervous I start to lecture like the world's number one bore. I'm trying to stop myself from telling you about the name Lutetia, an old Roman name for Paris that means swamp or marsh. Or maybe the other way around."

"When I'm nervous," Annie said, "I like to hear lectures."

Shaw shook his head, as if to say he didn't know what to say. Annie took his arm and they walked comfortably through the darkened streets, in and out of occasional patches of light from uncurtained windows. Once they paused to look at a street sign—"rue du Dragon"—and wondered idly what it could mean. "After all, here be no dragons," Annie said.

"But there be the river," Shaw said, although from where they stood they could only see a distant gleam that may or may not have been water.

The rain gave a last brisk whisk across the rooftops and went away. They passed along the rue Bonaparte, by the silent École des Beaux Arts, and finally emerged on a quai of the Seine, where people were still out and about and cars, civilian and military, were hurrying by in both directions. A cold wind whipped toward them from the water, a November wind that might have started far away in the east, in the Ardennes or Germany, some place where winter had already begun. When they reached the middle of the Pont des Arts and stopped, Annie decided it was time to talk again.

"I have no idea why they call them the Left Bank and the Right Bank," she said and waved her hand back and forth. "Why not the North and South Banks?"

"Because the first maps of Paris showed the city from the middle of the river, looking west, and so—"

"—so one was on the left, one was on the right. You really are the most boring date, Professor Shaw." But she laughed to show she was joking and took his arm again.

They leaned against the balustrade and faced upstream, toward the Pont Neuf, where some privileged street lamps made a high row of white dots. Behind it, riding toward them like the ghostly prow of a ship, loomed the great misty mass of gray that was Notre Dame.

"I saw your twin in Holland," Annie said. "The handsome Captain Adams."

"Ah." Shaw concentrated on the shadows moving along the surface of the water.

"I bet he was quite the ladies' man at Harvard." But if she hoped to provoke him, Shaw merely shrugged. "He corrected my prose," she said.

Shaw looked over and gave the grin that made him look like a nine-year-old boy. "Of course he did."

"He's just like Martha. I wrote that a bridge connects two worlds, and he pointed out that in Holland it was still the same country, therefore still the same world."

"A bridge does connect two worlds," Shaw said slowly as he turned toward her, "but only because something divides them."

Annie made the sharp little sound she had heard French women make at the end of sentences and she let him lean toward her and kiss her, not urgently, but softly, gently, and for a long time. She felt the Silver Star under his overcoat scratch her hand. A killer's kiss. *Au feeling.*

When his hand went lower, she let him squeeze her breast because she wanted to, but then pushed it abruptly away, because—

"I'm sorry," she said and stepped back so that a space divided them. "I'm really sorry. I know you're moving out soon—but I don't want to be just a foxhole fuck."

And the instant she said it, she regretted the awful vulgar phrase, the fucking military slang, and she saw a flicker of something pass over his face. Goddamned Harvard men. "I shouldn't talk like that."

"Hey, soldier! Break it up!"

At the end of the bridge on the Right Bank side, a jeep with hooded headlamps materialized out of the shadows and a white-helmeted Military Police sergeant swung out of the passenger seat. "Sorry, captain," he said. "Didn't see the bars. We got some kind of mob moving this way, anarchists, communists, vegetarians, I don't know, but we don't want you out on the streets."

"We're fine," Shaw said.

"No, sir, you're not. Gotta insist."

Annie cocked her head. Somewhere not far off she heard sirens. Then the pat-pat-pat of small arms fire and an explosion.

"Get in the back!" the sergeant yelled. They scrambled in and the jeep lurched into gear. When they came to a stop three minutes later in front of the Hôtel Scribe, Annie could still hear gunfire from the other side of the river. Shaw was leaning over the seat to look at the sergeant's map and pointing. She stepped awkwardly out, shook away the other MP's help, and touched Shaw's arm for a moment. Something exploded in the nearby Tuileries Garden.

"I'd better go," he said, and she could see in his eyes that the lover had turned back into the soldier.

Annie nodded and said, "Call me," but the jeep was already in gear again, starting to roll. "The horse knows the way," she added pointlessly, and then she walked to the door of the Scribe and listened to the sound of pistols and voices crying out and understood that she was hearing Eros and Thanatos, locked as always in a never-ending embrace.

# Three

In Versailles, General Eberhardt had a small private office next to his big conference room office. Nobody could quite figure out what the room had been used for in the seventeenth century, though Eberhardt liked to say it was obviously a hiding place for the king's number-two mistress. In honor of his own misspent youth at the University of Arkansas, he called it the "Razorback Lair." Adams thought it had probably been a privy.

"You judge a man in the army, Adams, by how many offices he has," Eberhardt said now, turning and gesturing with his coffee cup to show off the room. "Eisenhower has more offices than God."

"He has more soldiers, sir."

Eberhardt snorted and aimed the cup at a map of Germany hanging on the wall. "Three more maps under that one, on a roller. Turn us to Belgium, Major."

Adams did as he was told while Eberhardt lowered himself into a chair behind the desk and began a monotonous back and forth swivel that must have driven his law clients back in Little Rock crazy. "This not too late for you, son?"

Adams resisted the impulse to look at the wall clock above the general's bookcase. He already knew that it was past two in the morning and that it was a kind of laying on of hands to be invited into the Lair all by himself, no matter what time it was. He shook his head, which was morally preferable to an outright lie. It was ridiculously late.

"I like maps," Eberhardt said. "I've always liked maps. My wife says we have maps at home the way other houses have ants. See that stack over there?"

Adams saw it. A foot-high stack of topo maps in various black and green folio binders. There was another map hanging from the back of the door, and graphs, and oversized folders of the daily aerial photos the RAF distributed every morning.

"When I was a kid I used to draw maps of imaginary places. You know what the first map of an imaginary place was, Major?"

"*Treasure Island.*"

Eberhardt was not the kind of general who liked having his questions answered. He made the snorting sound again and pushed a manila folder across his desk. "Read this."

When Adams looked up again the general was standing in front of his map of Belgium. "This is where she was."

Eberhardt put his finger on a wavy line at the far eastern edge of Belgium that represented a river with the curious name of Our. "She" was the woman interviewed in the manila folder, Elise Dele, a forty-one-year-old German-speaking Luxembourger refugee who had been captured by the Germans and later picked up by the Americans, and whose interrogation, the general said, bothered the hell out of him.

On Eberhardt's wall map you could follow her story exactly. Three weeks ago she and her thirteen-year-old son had returned to their home in the village of Bivels, intending to collect warmer clothes for the winter. They were walking south alongside the

Our when a German patrol stopped them and forced them into a truck. They drove both of them blindfolded to a base at Bitburg, eighteen miles inside Germany, and questioned them for a day or so with routine German brutality about American installations. Then they took away her son and left her stranded in the country. Over the course of the next three days she made her way back to the Our, but found that the bridges connecting Germany to Belgium had been destroyed. She detoured north, stumbled into a line of German bunkers and artillery placement, and finally fell into the hands of the Belgian Resistance, who rowed her across the river and passed her over to the American 109th Infantry.

"The report says she saw German troops in light gray uniforms with black collars."

"SS," Eberhardt said. "They shouldn't be there. They should be way farther north. *Or* farther south."

"The 109th says she's too nervous and upset about her son to be believed."

"But *she* says she remembers the Germans coming through her town in 1916 and it looks just the same now—soldiers, trucks, artillery everywhere."

"Exactly where you said they might come again, the Ardennes." Adams ran his hand across the map. Eberhardt was known in Versailles to be a worrier, somebody who saw gremlins behind every shadow—Adams glanced again at the date on the folder—which was probably why the report had taken so long to reach his desk. But he was far from a fool.

Eberhardt picked up a red wax crayon and drew a great bulge from the German Border through eastern Belgium, straight west toward the sea. Then he sketched in big arrows representing the tracks that an armored division might take through the sparsely defended American lines. Then another red arrow coming up from the south toward the central Belgian town of Bastogne. An imaginary map with real soldiers in it.

"They're coming back," Eberhardt said.

# Four

ON THE LAST DAY OF NOVEMBER, ELECTRICITY WAS STILL OUT OF the question most of the day in Paris. Annie had tried working in her room at the Scribe, but without any light it was too cold and dark and lonely, so she had begun a new routine of writing at the Café des Matelots down the street, where at least there were candles at every table and people to look at when the words froze in her mind.

Besides, Martha had told her that Hemingway wrote everything in cafés. And besides again, sometimes the Matelots had real coffee to serve, not "muckefucke," or even worse, *gazeux,* which was a fake coffee made with carbonated water that tasted of streaky green chemicals. But there was never any pastry.

Before coming to the café this morning she had walked down the rue Saint-Honoré and stopped in front of the window at Rumplemeyer's, where there was only a cardboard cake in the window and a little sign that said "model." The clothing store next to it was closed, but had a cardboard "model" of a shoe in its window.

She shivered and swished aside the flap of her GI overcoat and studied her own boots, warm fur-lined brown army boots that

David Schuyler, back in town, had somehow liberated for her. Then she looked at the waiter behind the zinc who was poking morosely at the telephone, probably willing it to ring. But of course, there was no phone service either, at least for French civilians. She had twice used the American lines in the Scribe to call Shaw at his barracks in Versailles, but he hadn't gotten the message, or he was off to war again, or after she had pushed him away, he just wasn't interested.

She adjusted her tablet and pencil and squared them with the table, because any little ritual was better than actually trying to write when you were sitting in your overcoat in a half-dark room, freezing—Schuyler was ribald and fun and would have said "freezing your balls off." But he hadn't called back either. Nor had Adams, who was now *Major* Adams according to Martha, incredibly busy and rapidly climbing the greasy pole of promotion.

There was a woman sitting on the banquette opposite who also appeared to be writing something. She was short, dark, and as the French say, *pulpeuse,* and despite her frumpy clothes and unwashed hair she seemed to Annie simply to exude sex appeal. Something Annie couldn't describe just baked off her, some musk or vibration that had every man in the café turning restlessly toward her from time to time and staring and fidgeting with their collars. People called *her* back, Annie thought.

She looked at what she had written so far, which she judged in all fairness to be absolutely terrible—1500 flat, uninspired words on the Negro American singer Josephine Baker, who had just given a benefit concert for French widows and orphans. Waiting after the concert for an interview, Annie had met a colored army nurse who told her there were fifty of them—Negro nurses—in Paris, but they were only allowed to treat Negro soldiers or German POWs, never American whites, and she had briefly thought of writing about them instead. But British *Vogue* wouldn't want it and the Associated Press wouldn't want it, and she was just asking herself again why Schuyler and the Twins seemed immune to her own musk and vibration when the glass door of the café shattered into pieces.

What happened next didn't so much unfold as blow apart into nightmarish shards—a disc of short blonde hair, spurting blood—arms clawing over the floor toward her table—the woman on the banquette standing and silently screaming. Then a mob burst through the door and swarmed over the disc of blond hair that was in fact, Annie saw with horror, a teenaged boy, and there was a blur of legs and shoes and the boy crumpled and turned to red and bone as the legs kicked and stamped and the last thing Annie saw before she turned and vomited was a wooden shoe crushing his jaw and the last thing she heard was *"Pédé! Pédé!"*—which was French for homosexual—before she ran out into the street, where it was raining again.

LATER, IN HER COOL, MATTER-OF-FACT BRYN MAWR DRAWL, MARtha explained that the boy was undoubtedly a prostitute who had been in the business of servicing German soldiers, and the French, belonging to a Christian Catholic country, naturally despised his kind far more than the female *horizontales* and thought it was meet, right and their bounden duty to kick them all to death.

"Drink this."

She handed Annie a tumbler of Johnnie Walker scotch, chosen from the elaborate lineup of bottles on the apartment's handsome Louis XVI sideboard. Above the bottles rose shelf after shelf of foreign-looking books, all the way up to the ceiling. And behind the couch where Annie was sitting, more shelves, more books, and a charming collection of painted porcelain figurines, little Chinese girls in pigtails astride galloping ponies. The apartment was on the rue de Seine, not far from the Sorbonne, and belonged to a professor of Asian History who had known somebody that Martha had known in Spain and who had long ago fled to Portugal. Martha had the use of it for a week or so, because she was sick of the "ink slingers," as she put it, at the Scribe, and also because Hemingway, while keeping his room at the Ritz, had now also taken a room at the Scribe.

The apartment building had its own generator in the basement, so that there was a scratchy table lamp by the professor's reading chair and a still fainter one down the hall, in the bedroom. Martha went to the window, drew back the curtain, and frowned at the street below.

"He's supposed to blow his horn, but he's probably going to hoot three times like an owl or do something else Tom Sawyerish to let us know he's here. You OK? You still want to go?"

Annie nodded and swallowed more scotch. It was prewar strong, but she could still taste the vomit in her mouth. "I'm all right. I've seen worse things," she said, although she hadn't.

At eleven-thirty, another scotch later, they heard a car horn outside. When they reached the curb, an ancient Citroën C4 was idling loudly and a boy no older than the teenaged prostitute stood on the sidewalk, looking suspiciously up and down the empty black street. He wore a US Army greatcoat and ragged canvas shoes, and when he pulled the door open for them, he studied Annie's boots carefully for an envious moment or two. The driver, another boy, said nothing but revved the engine and glowered at the world.

The rain had stopped. Patches of fog hovered over the pavement, then whispered away in the dark as the car drove through them.

"Place d'Italie," Martha said. "In the Thirteenth."

The driver said nothing, but pumped the gearshift like a trombone and made a sharp turn left.

It was astonishing how lost you could get at night, when the streetlamps were far between and few and the winter sky pushed down on the city, heavy and black like a lid on a pan. Reflexively, Annie hunched her shoulders and squinted at what she took to be the plane trees of the Luxembourg Garden, where she knew there were lovely white marble statues of famous women ringing the sailboat pond and no boys were stomped to death.

"Place d'Italie," Martha said again, but this time it was not so much a direction to the driver as an announcement to Annie. "You know it?"

Annie did not. The place d'Italie was one of the dark, anarchic parts of liberated Paris, a center of purging and riots. Americans stayed away from it. But Martha had a contact, she said, another friend of a friend, and she had a lead for a *Collier's* story about the "secrets" of the Paris black market.

Annie didn't quite believe her. Martha Gellhorn wouldn't get in a car at midnight with two teenaged cowboys and go to the place d'Italie just to meet black marketers. You could meet black marketers in the corridors of the Scribe. Or maybe, being Martha, whose life was indistinguishable from theater, if it seemed like an adventure you did go.

"*À gauche*, turn left."

Five or fifteen minutes later—it was hard to keep track of time in the dark—they found themselves in another apartment, as unlike the one on the rue de Seine as possible. This one also had electricity, so a bare overhead bulb spread a haze of yellowish light over the living room, but instead of books and delicate porcelain figurines, Annie saw jerry cans of gasoline lined along the floor and heavy brown cardboard boxes with US Army stenciling. Other, flimsier boxes appeared to hold nylon stockings. Two more sullen boys lounged on a sofa. The rug was littered with cigarette butts and empty champagne bottles and what Martha would later call in her article "discarded erotica."

They stood in the center of the rug, directly under the light. Down the hall a door opened and Martha took out her notebook, and Annie suddenly understood why she hadn't been allowed to bring her camera.

"I'm Michel."

"Martha. Annie."

He said something to the boys in French, and when he turned back to them Annie realized that he had said "Michael" not "Michel" and he was American and he had the saddest face she had ever seen.

The boys stood up slowly, insolently, and sauntered out of the room. Michael looked hard at Annie. "You wait over there."

He guided Martha by the elbow to the couch—filthy red velvet with brass studs, Annie noted, as if she were writing the story, not Martha—and they sat down, heads close together, and began to talk in voices too soft and muffled for Annie to understand.

She took a few steps around the room, keeping her distance from them. More boxes of nylons, cans of motor oil, six cartons labeled "Spam." Despite herself, Annie made a little huff of laughter and tried to imagine what kind of joke Shaw would make about eating in a Three Spam Michelin restaurant. She looked carefully over toward the couch.

Michael was tall and skinny, with just the beginnings of a paunch visible under his sweater. It was, Annie recognized, an army sweater, a mechanic's sweater, ribbed gray cotton and brown leather collar and elbow patches. She had seen a thousand like it in motor pools from Normandy to Holland, and she had seen a thousand Michaels too, easy moving, slightly stooped at the shoulders, with one of those Adam's apples you find in some

Southerners, big and triangular like a Frenchman's nose. But from what she could hear, there was no Southern accent, just a faint adenoidal twang that seemed somehow unmistakably American.

What Michael was, she realized, was a deserter.

Annie stepped into the hallway that led to the kitchen and Michael looked up sharply. "That's off-limits, lady."

She turned back obediently. She had never seen a deserter before. Everybody knew they existed, nobody wrote about them. They were like the Negro nurses, invisible. Back home, every GI was brave like Shaw, or super-smart like Adams. Only Martha, irreverent Martha would have the gumption and maybe the pull to write about the cowards, the malingerers, the lily-livered traitorous Americans who cut and ran. And maybe not even Martha, because just at that moment Michael (if that was his name) abruptly stood up and whirled around as if somebody had slapped him and looked Annie square in the face.

If she had brought her camera, she could have snapped a picture to go along with her photograph of the women in Chartres. No shaved head in this picture, of course, no fidgeting infant or white stubbled scalp. Nobody had spat on Michael's face or drawn a swastika on his forehead in lipstick. But the camera would have captured the same stunned look, when the earth falls away under your feet, and the same ghostly pallor. And the next click of the shutter would have shown the tears running down Michael's cheeks.

"He wants me to help get him a *pardon*," Martha said. She stood up too. Her voice was absolutely acid with scorn.

"She knows generals," Michael muttered, "famous writers."

"He left his unit in Eindhoven, just ran away like a dog." Martha was gathering her things, her notebook, the overcoat she had taken off when they sat down.

"There's a whole prison of AWOLs out by Le Mans," Michael said. "Thousands of people, thousands." He spread his hands, as if pleading to Annie, who was still standing by the hallway, frozen with pity. "You can't put a man through that, what I went through, and then send him to prison."

"He's making a fortune," Martha said scornfully. "On the black market, stealing from his buddies."

She had reached the door and was pulling on her gloves. She gestured for Annie to join her. For what seemed like a long moment, long enough for Martha to stiffen with impatience, Annie hesitated. Some part of her mind, the journalist part, noted that in her own polished, brilliantly confident way, Martha was as unforgiving of weakness as her husband. But Martha lacked the warm, unconfident part that was Annie's gift, and that made her yearn to go to Michael and put her arms around him and sit down together with him till the hurt went away, though she already knew that it never would.

"He's a fucking coward," Martha said. Mechanically, like someone just waking up, Annie turned away from him and walked toward the door.

This was the third of the moments when her world fell to pieces. The fourth was still a long time to come.

# Five

In Versailles, General Eberhardt's history lessons continued.

The day after Annie's visit to the place d'Italie, Adams found
himself summoned to a staircase outside the *Cour Royale* and
then hustled downstairs and out into the cold. It was just past
four o'clock in the afternoon, a frigid, iron-gray December
afternoon that for some reason had made the contrarian Eberhardt think he would like to take a stroll in the king of France's
gardens. To beat the cold he was wearing an aviator's leather
jacket with a fleece collar and very prominent, very polished
silver stars on the shoulders, because Eberhardt was a man who
much enjoyed being a general.

"You know where the water for all these fountains comes
from, Major?"

Adams looked around helplessly. The hedges and trees were
gray, the sky was gray, the water in the gray fountains was gray.
He had no idea where the water came from.

"Machine de Marly," Eberhardt said. "Over those hills a couple of miles. Louis XIV had it built to pump water to the Palace.
Some kind of crazy hydraulic pump that took sixty men to run.

It broke down all the time and finally gave up for good in 1817, and now they use steam power. The French have never been any good with plumbing."

Eberhardt had spent most of the day in staff meetings with Eisenhower and Omar Bradley, and he invariably came back from these meetings fretting about some four-star stupidity or injustice. Invariably, he took his time getting around to what was bothering him.

"You know our terms for Germany, Adams?"

"Yes, sir. 'Unconditional surrender.'"

"Yep. Unconditional surrender." Eberhardt's voice was surprisingly flat. "Roosevelt announced it after Yalta. Churchill had no idea he was going to say that, but then of course Churchill had to go along. Stalin didn't give a shit." He stopped to pull the collar higher and sniff the late afternoon air. "Snow coming," he announced. "You know where that 'unconditional' stuff comes from?"

"I don't, sir."

"Ulysses S. Grant, the Yankee Butcher of Virginia. Those were the terms he offered Bobby Lee at Appomattox. You think it's a good idea?"

Adams frowned and scuffed his boot in the gravel path to buy time. He had no idea what Eberhardt wanted him to say. "I guess it's a good idea."

"It's a *horrible* idea," Eberhardt said. "Think about it, son. Think about the casualties. We're sitting on the fucking German border right now. For all intents and purposes the war's over. We could negotiate a peace. We don't have to kill another quarter million boys, just to prove we've won. The smart Germans already know it."

"They're fanatics, sir."

Eberhardt sighed and pulled out a cigar. "Yeah. And we're not," he said in the same dead, flat voice.

They walked almost to the end of the endless gardens, mostly in silence. Near the Petit Trianon, Eberhardt stopped to explain that the quite grand classical building in front of them had once been Marie Antoinette's "cottage," where she liked to dress as a shepherdess and tend sheep. They leaned against a cross-rail fence that must have once enclosed the royal ruminants and looked back at the enormous palace. The soldiers going back and forth around the grounds looked tiny, like ants. Sometimes, Adams thought, only a cliché will do.

"What I don't like is all the radio silence," Eberhardt said. "It's like the dog that didn't bark."

And now they had reached it, the thing that was bothering him—Eberhardt's continuing fear that despite the winter lull, despite the fact that the German army was reeling, they still had strength enough for one great, last counterattack. And odds were, he told everybody who would listen, it would come in *his* sector. Nobody, nobody at all in authority, agreed.

On the other hand, in the matter of radio silence, Adams saw his point. Normally their office saw reams of daily intercepted German radio signals, most of them in code. A lot of the signals, he had figured out, were somehow interpreted by an extremely secret unit either in France or—he guessed—England. The mathematician in him was curious about how so many codes could be so quickly broken. But since the interrogation report on the Luxembourger woman Elise Dele, they had received almost no interceptions from the area running roughly south from the German city of Aachen to the Luxembourg border.

A very cautious American lieutenant in the Belgian city of Bastogne had reported two more panzer divisions assembled just across the border. But he had couched the report in such cautious, uncertain language that Eberhardt's superiors, optimistic, comfortable, enjoying the prospect of unconditional surrender, dismissed the warnings out of hand. Germany was beaten. In the spring the Allies would march more or less unopposed into Berlin.

Eberhardt was looking at him curiously. "You don't mind about the casualties, do you, Major?"

That was unfair. Adams looked at the distant palace and tried to think of a proper answer.

"You think strategically, not tactically, don't you, Major? You don't worry about the men that much."

Adams decided on the one answer that never got you in trouble in the army. "Sir."

"Say you were Hitler," Eberhardt persisted. "What would you be doing, right here, strategically?" He knelt, picked up a twig, and in Marie Antoinette's beautifully raked gravel, drew wavy lines for the Rhine and the Our rivers, a dot for Luxembourg City, a dot for Aachen, where, because it was on the soil of the Fatherland, the Germans had made a murderous stand in September as part of the Hürtgen Forest offensive; another dot for Bastogne in central Belgium.

"Strategically," Eberhardt said, "you don't just counterattack for the hell of it. You have a *goal,* you have a place you want to end up."

Adams knelt beside him and studied the lines and dots. Strategy was just geometry with guns. After a moment he picked up his own twig and added a dot and a crescent, Atlantic-facing, on the left side of Bastogne. "Antwerp," he said. "Antwerp Harbor. That's a goal. If you attacked east to west, straight through Bastogne, you'd reach the Meuse River and split us in half and own one of the biggest harbors in Europe."

Eberhardt held the twig lengthwise like a ruler and rubbed east to west until he wiped out Bastogne and reached Antwerp. "And before you attacked, you'd go on radio silence and you'd mass your people just beyond the Our River and then go right through the Ardennes to the sea," he said. "The same route Hitler went in 1940, and before that in 1916, when he was a snot-nosed little corporal in the German army. You know what Mark Twain said about history, Major?"

Adams was beginning to think he didn't know much. "No, sir."

LATER THAT DAY, HE FOUND OUT.

"He said history doesn't repeat itself," Shaw told him. "But it *rhymes.*"

Adams poured the last drops of wine from the bottle and reached across the table for the other bottle they had ordered. "You and the learned general."

"There's another reason he might go through the Ardennes," Shaw said. He paused, evidently waiting to be asked. Adams decided that he loved Shaw like a brother, but he was getting tired of him.

"It's all forest," Shaw said. "Like the Hürtgen Forest."

"So what?"

"The Germans and *forests,* B. T.—in German mythology forests are dangerous, full of goblins and wolves and good-looking Aryan gods with hammers. Think about Wagner, *Grimm's Fairy Tales.* Only the pure of heart and race can get safely through a forest. That's Hitler. The weak, the impure—that's us—we're done for."

"That," Adams said carefully, "is bullshit. Captain."

"Probably." Shaw pulled the bottle back to his side of the table. "Plays well with others. Shares," he said in their old bantering manner and filled his glass. "Why do you think Hitler calls himself the 'Fürher'?"

"It means 'Leader,'" Adams said.

"It means 'Guide.'"

Adams leaned back and looked around the room. There were so many American soldiers in Versailles now that most of the officers had been moved out of the temporary barracks and tents and installed in local hotels. He and Shaw had been assigned to the Hôtel de la Reine, which featured dozens of portraits of Marie Antoinette in the lobby and a tiny restaurant called "Regina." After dinner Shaw had insisted, in honor of the unlucky queen, on ordering an enormous slice of cake. They were roommates again, just as at Harvard. But they weren't at Harvard anymore.

"He lives in underground bunkers," Shaw said, beginning to slur his s's, the way he did when he drank too much. "Like a wolf. And all his houses have 'wolf' in their name—Wolf's Lair, *Wolfsschanze*. I thought you studied German. Hitler's the wolf-guide who can get them safely through the forest, the Hürtgen Forest in this case, and surprise us all."

Adams drummed his fingers on the table. "You know you'd be laughed out of any staff meeting."

"You mean I don't think *strategically* like you."

"We never do think alike."

"'Adolf,'" Shaw said, "is an old German name that means 'wolf.'" He finished his wine and turned his attention to his plate. "Let us eat cake."

Upstairs the room they shared was so small that the two beds were only a foot or so apart. Adams expected Shaw to continue his slightly tipsy professorial lectures until he fell asleep, on wolves or queens or even that reliable old bore Thomas Jefferson. But Shaw had gone strangely quiet. All he said as he climbed into bed was, "Hell of a thing, go to war in pajamas."

For some minutes they lay silently, side by side, hearing each other breathe and swallow. Somebody's platoon trotted down the street at double time. A single airplane droned overhead, far away.

Inevitably it began to rain, dot after dot against the window, foreign rain, French rain. Rain was general all over France. "I saw that Annie March in Holland," Adams said.

Shaw said nothing, but Adams could tell by his breathing that he was still awake. "I know," Shaw said finally. "She told me."

Adams turned and propped himself on one elbow. "I like her a lot," he said.

No sound except the rain.

"I'm going to see her again."

Shaw said nothing.

"So keep the fuck away," Adams said half to himself. He stared at the window and clenched and unclenched his fist and waited for sleep to come.

# Six

THE NEXT MORNING, DECEMBER 2, ALL FURLOUGHS FOR ENLISTED men in the 101st Airborne were cancelled. Meaning, as nobody needed to be told, that regrouping after Market Garden was finished. Meaning also, as nobody needed to be told, that they would almost certainly be going east, toward Germany and combat again.

Enlisted men's leaves were canceled, but not officers'. That night Shaw read the orders twice to be sure, then went to the cramped closet under the stairs that the Hôtel de la Reine mistook for a telephone booth and placed a call to the Scribe. Mlle. March was not in. With their compliments, Reception would give her the message.

He hung up with the gut-turning feeling of being underhanded and deceptive—he could see Adams at the bar, drinking brandy with a red-faced Colonel Blimp—angry with himself, angry with the goddam army that wouldn't let the war end. His headaches were coming back. But he wouldn't keep the fuck away from Annie March.

Outside, the French rain had finally wept itself to sleep. But the weather wasn't over. Here and there a few snowflakes floated in the wind and the air had a crisp, brittle feeling that made him think of the winter that was already well underway in Germany, in Belgium. He smoked half a cigarette he didn't want and watched a bus full of recruits rattle by on the road to their barracks. They would be going east in a day or so, too. A grotesque fantasy elbowed its way into his brain—what if Eisenhower or Montgomery or Bradley, sitting on their godly non-combatant perches, knew the future? What if at the start of a battle they gave every recruit a ribbon—green meant you would survive, red you would die. Yellow meant you would run away. You pinned on your ribbon and you picked up your rifle like a soldier.

He shook his head and thought of Annie March's face when he had kissed her, and her breasts, and her legs. He was tired, and from Normandy on he had done those things he ought not to have done, and there was no health in him, and in some black, untouchable part of his heart he almost hoped he hadn't picked a green ribbon. He thought the hell with his best friend and twin.

THE NEXT MORNING HE LEFT THE HOTEL AT FOUR-THIRTY A.M. AS usual, an hour before Adams was even awake, and set out on foot, solitary, through the dark foreign streets. One full day at the barracks was the plan. One last night in Paris.

The Versailles that tourists saw was Adams's Versailles—the château, the King's Tennis Court, the famous gardens of Le Nôtre and the Petit Trianon. Shaw's Versailles was farther north in the countryside, where part of the 101st was garrisoned in an old French army engineering camp. When you left the Hôtel de la Reine in the city center you passed through a rigid grid of streets that had been first laid out by one of the Louis kings—Shaw couldn't remember which one; as an anti-royalist Jeffersonian he didn't care. The grid was meant to symbolize the rigid, absolute power of the monarch.

But you soon exited what he thought of as the king's paw-print and entered a space of open fields and normally human, normally confusing and unplanned roads that climbed quickly in elevation and turned into doughy French hills. The garrison occupied most of a ridge two miles west of the pawprint, over-looking a bowl-shaped parade ground that was often filled, as it was this morning, with a trough of clammy white fog that moved and shifted with the breeze, like a living, breathing thing. Shaw thought of wolves and forests and shivered.

It was never really quiet in an army garrison. Already work details policed the paths between buildings. Men with croaky morning voices and bulky winter gear were lining up at the mess hall, stamping their boots against the chill. Down in the parade ground, shouts bounced and echoed. In the motor pool some-body raced an engine.

Other company captains let their sergeants supervise the morning routine, but the Puritan in Shaw thought that was shirk-ing a duty. His habitual practice was to rotate among the platoons, ostensibly to oversee the work, in fact to study his people. And in the First Platoon barracks there was already a problem.

A paratrooper jumped with a minimum amount of equip-ment—rifle, ammunition, mess kit and canteen, first aid kit. Most men tied grenades to their belts and stuffed their jumpsuits with socks and cigarettes. Everything else that they needed was to be packed in what the airborne army, moving in its mysterious way, called a "seaborne" roll. This was to be handed over to trans-port and delivered to the front, when the front was, in another military assault on the language, "static."

The problem was that half the men in First Platoon were poorly trained replacements—"one day jumpers"—and had no idea how to pack a seaborne. In the middle of the barracks a sergeant had spread out a shelter half on the floor. When Shaw entered, he was folding a blanket on top of it and demonstrating how to fill it with gear and tie it with a length of tent rope that could double as a shoulder strap.

But the private nearest Shaw, a nineteen-year-old Georgian named Driskell, had crammed so much into his roll that the ends of the rope wouldn't meet, and if the kid wasn't crying with frustration, he was so close to it that Shaw knelt beside him and started repacking.

"The thing is, soldier, the roll can't be more than thirty inches long and a foot in diameter."

"Yes, sir. But I got to take my Bible. And this sweater my sister made. Got to have it."

A few feet away the First Sergeant looked up at Shaw and shook his head.

"The Bible's OK." Shaw pulled the sweater out of the pile and tossed it aside. The kid yelped in protest and Shaw fixed him with a stare. *The sergeant can be their friend. The captain can't.* "But not the sweater, not these pants, not this either."

"Dammit, sir!"

*Got*, Shaw remembered. The word that ate English according to the gospel of Martha. *Got* to take my Bible. For a moment of horrifying clarity he saw Driskell's future—jagged ends of splintered bone, a stump of flesh, a falling cadence of breath. A blood red ribbon. "And everything has to be marked with your name. Sergeant, give him a stencil."

Shaw came to his feet and went on to the next man, who was also trying to pack all his worldly goods into the seaborne. It was mostly pointless, as Shaw and the "old men"—the kids who had already been in combat—knew. Half the time the seaborne roll would never reach the front. And if it did, it had usually been looted by the jerkoffs in transport who stole flashlights, money, sweaters, cigarette lighters, anything they thought they could use or sell. He thought of Wilcox. He thought of a hundred other Wilcoxes. He thought of the Latin inscription on the Boston Common monument to his Civil War ancestor, Robert Gould Shaw. *Relinquunt Omnia Servare Rem Publicam.* "They gave up everything to serve the State."

If the Germans started seriously shooting again, Driskell would be dead before breakfast.

COMPANY D ATE LUNCH AT ELEVEN, AND HALF AN HOUR LATER was back in the barracks, finishing their seabornes, working on the musette bags of toiletries that everybody hooked onto their packs. Shaw watched Driskell and five or six of his buddies, all replacements, all of them younger than twenty, all (in the view of the old men) dumb as a box of rocks.

The old men, of course, had trained at Fort Benning, a grueling twelve-week ordeal that flunked out eighty per cent. The new kids were products of Montgomery's inability to use paratroopers correctly, just as Adams had said in Holland. For Monty, paratroopers were infantry, not first strike assault teams. After Market Garden, to flesh out the airborne units decimated by that boneheaded policy, he made things worse by ordering that anybody at all could join the "Troops." The only requirement for the new boys was to make three jumps in one day. No three months of thirty-hour days and endless tactical drops. Their chutes were packed for them by civilian women. They jumped without battle packs, over wide, treeless meadows. Shaw thought he had seen circus rides more dangerous. The old men thought Montgomery was a murderer.

After Driskell failed the third time to field strip his M-1, Shaw ordered the replacements from all three platoons out to the parade ground. There he and two sergeants trotted them around the big field for twenty minutes straight, packs on, rifles ready. Then when they were good and winded, he set them marching double time for another half hour, while he stood off to one side with a stopwatch, wondering what Annie March was doing, wondering if he hated Adams, or feared him, or simply wanted to hold Annie March so close and tight that their hearts would crack. A foxhole fuck would be just fine.

"*I got a girl in Thomasville,*" the sergeants chanted. "*She won't blow me, but her sister will!*"

Most of the boys were too out of breath to sing anymore. Boots started to drag. Legs trembled. Shaw looked up at the low scudding clouds. Their bellies sagged, full of rain, and like a fool he remembered a truly stupid line from a Chekhov play and almost laughed—"I cannot approve of our climate."

"Break 'em down," he ordered, and the sergeants took off like cats, snatching rifles, breaking them open, scattering parts on the damp grass.

"One minute! Go!"

On their knees, bent double under their packs, the new men groped and scrambled and snapped the rifles back together. Some finished in thirty seconds. Some took the full minute. Driskell was still fumbling with the breech when Shaw knelt beside him, took the rifle out of his hands, and broke it apart again.

"One minute, Driskell. *Go!*"

It took two more tries before Driskell could put his rifle together in under a minute. When he looked up at Shaw, still kneeling beside him, there was no triumph in his eyes. His face was flushed, the tendons in his cheeks stood out like wires. His fingers were muddy, grass-stained, bleeding at the nails.

"Why you fucking hate me, Captain?"

Officers don't touch enlisted men, but Shaw did, all the time. He braced both hands on the kid's bony shoulders. "Love doesn't work so well, Driskell, out here."

He pushed himself to his feet and heard his knees crack like an old man's. For an instant the sky and clouds swam around him, and he thought that must be what it's like, at the end. The world swims, and flickers, and is gone.

# Seven

TWENTY-TWO MILES AWAY, IN THE HEART OF THE LEFT BANK, Martha took Annie's arm and steered her away from the crowd still exiting the Théâtre du Vieux-Colombier.

"I am under the impression," Martha said in her driest voice, "that I am having a damned good time in Paris."

"Nobody better."

Over her shoulder Martha scowled at the theatre marquee: "*Huis Clos* de Jean-Paul Sartre—*Reprise Matinée*."

"But after an hour of Sartre's philosophical gloomth I feel like taking a shower in disinfectant and then slitting my throat. Look at them," she added, making Annie stop and look back. "They should be too depressed to move, but there they are, chattering and bleating like existential sheep."

"Hell is other sheep," Annie said, parodying the play's best line, and Martha burst out in a laugh so loud that people stared.

"You're a very clever girl. What do you hear from the ardent Twins?"

"Oh, Martha."

"*Oh, Martha*, my eye. Tell Mummy."

137

Annie glanced at Martha, who seemed more elegant, more *Parisienne* than ever, if a *Parisienne* wore tailored khaki trousers and a leather aviator jacket and a heavy-lidded, half-weary pout that seemed to draw men like moths to a candle. Some "Mummy." Moths in a candle, of course, went up in flames. She looked at her watch. Three-thirty.

"I know Captain—now *Major*—Adams calls you at the Scribe."

"We had dinner once."

"Of course you did, and that was all."

"And that was all."

"We cross down there." They had passed the Hôtel Lutetia, which Martha had now turned against, and they were going to a writing and editing session in a café on the rue du Cherche-Midi, a new "burrow" more to her liking.

"What I don't understand, dear, wholesome Annie, virtually every other girl in Paris is giving it away for a pack of cigarettes and here you are playing hard to get with two delicious young officers. Who, astonishingly, seem to put up with it. You know," Martha added with Sartre-like cheerfulness, "they could both go off and be blown to pieces tomorrow."

Martha's regular table was next to the stove, though like most stoves in liberated Paris it was burning only a feeble mixture of newspaper and kindling and gave off about as much warmth as a matchstick. The men at the zinc bar were little heads in heavy black coats and looked like beetles. The waiter wore wool gloves with the fingertips cut off. Annie spread out her papers and then, like every writer in the world except Martha, tried to avoid writing. The café window was thickly curtained against the cold, but she could still see part of the street with the wonderful name— Cherche-Midi—"Search for Midday." But there was no sun. The street was gray, the pedestrians going past were exhaling icy white commas of breath, and the air itself looked frozen and brittle. She wondered what supremely hopeful poet had come up with the name.

And then by an association of ideas, she asked, "How did Captain Shaw win his medal?"

Martha was running a red pencil across one of Annie's sentences. She was editing Annie's latest article and Martha took corrections and revisions extremely seriously. She didn't lift her head from the paper. "In Normandy. He stormed a pillbox and captured eleven Germans and shot God knows how many more." She scowled at the line she had just deleted and wrote "stet" in the margin. "Anybody else would have shot the prisoners, too. Normandy was just horrible."

Annie continued to stare at the street. "Shaw wouldn't have."

Martha stopped writing and sat back. The waiter had brought them two *petits blancs* because that was Martha's regular order and that was what writers did, she said, to prime the pump. Annie knew it was what Hemingway did. Martha took her first swallow of the wine and smiled a tight, guarded smile that did nothing to hide the pain in her eyes.

"Good for you," she said. "Good for you, Annie. You found what you were looking for."

Annie flushed. To be doing something, she picked up her *petit blanc* as well. "He's coming tonight," she said. "To dinner at the Scribe. It's his last night before they leave." She paused. "I'm not a prude. I'm going to sleep with him," she told the tabletop.

A long pause. "I may have made a tiny blunder," Martha said.

In Versailles at three-thirty Shaw was at the motor pool inspecting the trucks that were going to carry them out in the morning. He had grown up riding in his father's 1932 Hudson, which had leather seats, a polished mahogany dashboard, and a handy-man chauffeur with a little peak cap to drive it on Sun-day. The trucks were a little different ride. The men called them "cattle vans," because they consisted of a flat, open-topped trailer, forty-feet long and pulled by a tractor cab, and they were fitted, not with leather seats, but with wood-slatted sidewalls and uphol-stered with loose straw on the floor. On a long ride you peed out the back. If you had to do more than pee, you used your helmet, which was then called your "thundermug." Fifty men to a trailer was the regulation. Often the men would start "Mooing" if an officer drove by in his jeep.

He slipped a clipboard from its peg to write something up and thought of Major Barrack in Holland, who had stepped off into eternity with a clipboard in his hand. The second truck had tires so bald you could toboggan on them, so he made a note on the motor pool status form, which was conscientious but point-less. There weren't any spare tires because the black market had gobbled them up, fresh off the boat.

"Bad news about your jeep, Captain."

This was a motor pool corporal named Bender, who had set aside a jeep for Shaw to pick up at five-thirty that afternoon. Shaw lowered the clipboard and turned around with a sinking feeling in his stomach.

"All leaves canceled, Cap."

"No, only for enlisted men."

"Officers, too, sir. They changed it. Just came down." Bender couldn't quite hide his satisfaction. He held out a mimeographed sheet of paper. "Jeeps are already being packed to go."

Shaw looked at his watch. "That must be a mistake."

"No, sir. Officers, too, sir." Bender snapped the mimeo with his finger. "See it right there? *Everybody* in the 101st got to stay on base tonight."

"I MAY HAVE MADE A TINY BLUNDER," MARTHA REPEATED.

Annie sat back, too, so that they were shoulder to shoulder, facing straight ahead. "What did you do?"

"My husband invited me to dinner at the Scribe tonight," Martha said. Annie frowned at the word "husband." Martha had a thesaurus of colorful terms for Ernest Hemingway, few of them printable, many of them beginning with "shit," but not the simple word "husband."

"He wants to *talk*." Martha finished her wine and slapped eight francs on the table, which was too much. "About a *reconciliation*," she said. "And I'm such a fool I said yes, *on condition* that you and your Major Adams be there too. Because." She stood up abruptly and clutched her papers protectively to her chest. "Because if you're there maybe he won't make a *fucking scene*," she said, and glowered at the men by the zinc, who were looking around curiously at the loud American woman. "Baby, I thought *Adams* was the one you liked."

Annie stood up too and jammed her papers into her folder. "It's Shaw's last night in Paris. I'm sorry."

"Weren't you listening? He wants a *reconciliation*."

"You," Annie said, and was surprised to hear how much her voice shook, "are impossible." She was about to say more, because she had just opened herself to Martha and made herself vulnerable, and especially after the deserter episode she should have known that Martha was a hard person, an egotistical person, an awful person and she thought it would be very easy to hate Martha. But she said none of those things because for the first and only time she could remember Martha was crying.

"Oh, for Christ's sake, Martha."

Martha wiped her eyes and fumbled with the zipper on her jacket.

"Oh, for Christ's sake. What time did you tell him?"

"Six. He likes to start early. So he can drink more."

Annie pulled back her sleeve to see her watch, a clunky, decidedly unfeminine Bulova that her hopeless father had given her at graduation. Ten minutes to five. He had given an identical one to her bemused mother. "Husband" was apparently not such a simple word.

"Just one glass, Martha. Then you'll have to take care of Major Adams yourself."

# Eight

THE FIRST THING ERNEST HEMINGWAY SAID TO ANNIE WAS, "I thought you were bringing a camera."

B.T. Adams came quickly to his feet, smiling broadly, and before she could react one way or the other he put a hand on her right hip and kissed her on the cheek.

"This is Annie." Martha managed to look both pleading and defiant. "She said she could stay for two drinks."

"Then here's the first one." Hemingway had a bottle of Hennessy cognac in front of him. He took his empty water glass, poured it full to the brim, and pushed it across the table to Annie.

"Ernest," B.T. said, "has been telling us about the fighting in the Hürtgen Forest last month."

"He's just come back to Paris, getting over pneumonia," Martha said.

Annie's mind was miles away. She glanced around the Scribe's dining room, the "Grand Café," and remembered that the first time she had seen it, in August, there were no clients, no food, a dim, sad space. Now even at the early hour of six p.m. the room was full of noisy gray-haired senior officers and their "nieces." She felt hollow. She had a headache from all the cigarette smoke. Her fingers in her lap kept folding and unfolding the note the receptionist had just given her.

She made an effort. "In the newspaper pictures I saw, Mr. Hemingway, you had an enormous beard. But now...."

Hemingway grinned and tapped his moustache with an index finger. "That was back in combat, at Aachen. I looked like a Cossack. When the Krauts are lobbing grenades at you, not much time for shaving."

"*Combat,*" Martha muttered sardonically, too softly for anyone but Annie to hear.

"I was just explaining to your boyfriend." Hemingway began arranging salt and peppershakers, forks and knives in battle formation on the tablecloth.

"Annie has lots of boyfriends," Martha said quickly.

Her husband looked at her unpleasantly. "Don't you all?"

Hemingway was forty-five years old, a big man, graying, "bearlike," as everybody said. With his shoulders hunched forward and tense, he gave off an unmistakable air of intimidation, but his voice, to Annie's surprise, was not a growl but a cultivated, pleasant Midwestern baritone. "This is where we attacked, across the river, into the trees, straight into Germany. We were the first Yanks to cross the Rhine."

While he spoke and B. T. nodded, Martha finished her own drink and signaled to a waiter. Hemingway looked over, annoyed, and raised his voice. "You should have read my dispatches, sweetheart. That's how you write about war, no sentimental guff, no stories about women on the home front." He refilled his brandy glass and recited, apparently from memory, "The infantry started coming back dragging a few wounded, some limping. You know how they look coming back. Then the tanks started coming back and the TDs coming back and the men coming back plenty. They couldn't stay in that bare field and the ones who weren't hit started yelling for the medicos, which always excites everybody.'"

He broke off and gulped brandy. "Ernest," Martha said. "Enough booze."

"Drunk, drunker, drunkest," Hemingway said and turned to Adams. "Boozo, ergo sum. How's your Latin, kid?"

"Ancient history."

"And where's your medal? I thought you had the Silver Star." Hemingway shifted in his chair to look at Annie. "They don't give those things away, you know. You have to do something—"

"Heroic," Martha interrupted.

Hemingway looked at her with pure dislike. "I was going to say 'gruesome.' Don't *ever* try to choose my words."

The waiter deposited another round of drinks, and B.T. squeezed Annie's hand. "This is going to be horrible," he whispered. "Please stay."

But Annie was already on her feet. "I have an awful headache," she said, which was true. "I'm so sorry," which was not. She smiled at Hemingway, who was glowering at his drink. "Next time I'll bring my camera."


THE ENTRANCE HALL OF THE SCRIBE HAD BEEN DESIGNED WHEN European public spaces were meant to be impressive and interminable. The general effect was of acres of marble, mahogany, and crystal, with touches of brassy gold here and there on the door handles and stair rails. A chandelier that had somehow survived the Liberation hung over a huge Persian rug in the lobby, though the effect of luxurious grandeur was somewhat undercut by the sleeping soldiers on the couches and the cases of K rations stored next to the reception desk.

Annie walked past them and down the corridor leading to the bar. Just to be doing something, she stopped and looked at the faded photographs on the wall—evidently the Lumière brothers, early inventors of a motion picture camera, had shown their first films in the Grand Café, in December 1895 according to the captions, so somebody had rescued half a dozen old stills from the films and labeled them "The Birth of Cinema."

She had looked at the photographs twenty times before, at first with what she thought of as professional interest, then with a kind of historical curiosity she had probably inherited from her father. The earliest motion pictures in France were very short, less than a minute long, and were called *actualities*, "daily life." One of the stills showed a blacksmith hammering. Another showed workers leaving a factory. No pictures of war. No pictures of humiliated women or homosexuals kicked to death. *Daily life has changed a bit*, she thought.

Like the needle of a compass, her mind went back to Shaw, to Shaw's canceled leave, the fucking army, pardon her French, and the fucking war. Captain Shaw was going back to the front to do gruesome and heroic things, and before he left she had wanted to give herself to him, because she could, because the other men she had seen, in London and after, were just flirtations, part of the craziness, and Martha was right. She had found what she was looking for. Or it felt like that. The last photograph on the wall showed a young woman in one of those head-to-toe bathing outfits smiling and plunging into the ocean.

In the bar she took a corner table and sat by herself, with her back to the door. She drank two scotches and ate a corned beef sandwich and was not at all surprised when, at about twenty minutes past seven, Martha slid into the chair next to her.

"He's not coming, is he?"

Annie shrugged and smiled at the wall. "Everybody in his battalion had their leave canceled. My virtue is safe." She put the receptionist's note on the table and smoothed it out with her fingers. "He says they move out at six in the morning, but he doesn't know where. Of course, he couldn't tell me anyway."

Martha picked up Annie's glass and sniffed. Her own fingers were trembling. "Scotch. I want some scotch. How come B.T. isn't moving out, too?"

Annie looked at her carefully. Martha's face was far more expressive, strictly speaking, than beautiful. It was her animation that made her so attractive, seductive. But right now her face was as animated as a tombstone. She wasn't interested in Shaw, Annie thought, or B.T. or anybody that was moving out. She was in her own place, out of reach, curled up in pain.

"He's not in the same battalion anymore," Annie said, but Martha had already twisted around and pantomimed an order to the barman. Then she fell uncharacteristically silent until her drink came.

"Mr. Johnnie Walker," she said, wrapping both hands around the glass, "*mon amigo*, just in the nick of time. I never want to touch brandy again in my life. Maybe he'll sneak away and come meet you anyway, go AWOL for the night."

Annie shook her head.

Martha sipped her whisky without appearing to taste it. "But no," she said, "I forget. Our Captain Shaw won't leave his men. Too damned dedicated and principled. You know what happened in there? He called a couple of his drunken pals over to the table and started telling them how bad I was in bed and then he asked one of them to go find Mary Welsh. He never wanted to talk about a reconciliation, he just wanted to punch me around a little." There was a tear in a corner of her eye, but it looked like a stone. "Isn't it fun being a girl?"

"What did B.T. do?"

"Nothing. What could he do? Maybe he was starstruck. You know that was all malarkey he was talking—being in combat, lobbing grenades." She lowered her voice to mock Hemingway's. "*'The ones who weren't hit started yelling for the medicos.'* The army wouldn't let him get near any real fighting, they don't want to see the famous writer blown up on their dime."

Martha had a number of ways of being drunk. Booze cannot stale my infinite variety, she had once told Annie. Tonight she was neither maudlin nor angry nor staggering the way she had been with William Walton. Tonight she was fluent, curiously abstract. "I only want not to be married anymore," she said quietly. She was turned partially away, facing the corridor to the lobby. "I want to be free, I want to be so free that the atom can't be freer, I want to be free like nothing quite bearable."

Abruptly she dropped into a mutter. "What happened to the fine gilded hopes when one expected to be like other people, with a place to come back to, someone to trust? I write like someone screaming, my articles are horrible and unread and inefficient. I don't even know what I'm screaming against, except maybe human cruelty." She lifted her glass. "*Fiat* kindness. Let there be kindness."

There was more of this, at least another four inches of whiskey more. Annie stopped paying attention. She too watched the door to the lobby, hoping that the army had opted for kindness, but thinking that Martha was right, he wouldn't leave his men, wishing he would.

"You have nice hips," Martha said suddenly. "Pronounced hips."

"Martha."

"B.T. told me it was your figure that nailed him, and that little overbite, but you don't have very big breasts and those glasses…." Martha shook her head.

"Martha, go to bed."

"Hips are what seduce men," Martha said. "Hips are for carrying children."

"I'm going upstairs," Annie said. She stood up and shoved some coins under her glass. "Promise me you'll go to bed. Promise you won't go back in there and find him."

"I have had two abortions," Martha said. "The first time was in January 1931, in Chicago. My father was furious. It was a married man and he wouldn't leave his wife. My father said, 'There are two kinds of women, and you're the other kind.' The second was in the summer of 1933, in Paris. I paid for it myself."

Annie remained on her feet, uncertain whether to go or stay. Martha smiled a quite horrible smile. "It's a world bursting with sin and sorrow, *n'est-ce pas?*"

IT WAS ANOTHER HALF HOUR BEFORE ANNIE FINALLY GOT AWAY and made her way to her room. Automatically, she turned on the light as she entered, absurdly she took a quick step toward the bed, as if John Michael Shaw might have magically appeared on it, grinning his kid grin, waiting for her.

But there were only the four cold walls, the dishonest French radiator, the wobbly little writing desk she had lugged up to the fourth floor by herself. She took off her dress and changed into a sweater two sizes too big and a pair of GI fatigue pants. While she fumbled with the maddening six-button fly she remembered the nurse at Chartres who had shown her how to replace the buttons with a zipper, but of course she had never gotten around to doing it, one more thing to add to her list of inadequacies, like her figure, her glasses. She cocked her head at the photograph of her mother and father on the desk. She was just like her father. All those things she had meant to learn and hadn't—how to sew, how to tie twenty kinds of knots, how to play the banjo... "My articles are unread and inefficient," Martha had said. Strange, strange word to choose—"inefficient." Isn't it fun being a girl?

She wondered about the GIs in the field, struggling to button themselves up while the bullets flew. If he did come tonight, would Shaw be wearing the same kind of pants? Would she get to unbutton them? She felt herself smile a wicked smile. Sometimes it *was* fun, being a girl.

Her clunky old Bulova watch said nine-fifteen, a ridiculously early hour to be in her room, alone, in Paris, cold. She sat on the bed with her knees pulled up and felt the slick condensation on the wall against her back, even through the sweater. Cold air slipped under the curtains and busied itself around the room, flipping through the papers on the desk, whispering in the corners. She assumed it was just as cold where Shaw was and she hoped against hope that he would break all the rules and love not honor more and steal away from the army and come to her, come to her bed.

At ten o'clock there were sporadic sounds of gunfire somewhere out in the city. She rewound the Bulova and turned off the light. If he hadn't come by eleven, she thought, closing her eyes, she would give it up.

At eleven she wound the Bulova again. If he hadn't come by midnight, she thought, she would give it up.

She was dozing, still sitting up in the bed with her arms wrapped around her knees, when she heard a loud rap-rap-rap that sounded like her door. But when she hurried to open it, the corridor was gray in the dim light, empty as air.

At one o'clock she dragged out her own bottle of *amigo* Johnnie Walker from her kit and drank just enough to make her sleepy. If he came by two o'clock, that would still leave him time enough to get back to Versailles, or wherever he was now.

But at three in the morning she still wasn't sleepy and she knew he wasn't coming. She opened the curtains and looked down at the rue Scribe, where the flags over the hotel entrance were snapping angrily back and forth in the cold east wind.

She looked at her watch again, which had Roman numerals on the dial, which made her think of Shaw, on his way east, back to the war, so a little tipsy now she drank more Scotch and thought boozo, *ergo sum. Amo, ergo sum.* Good for you, Annie, you found what you were looking for, and then you lost it.

She fell asleep staring at the door.

# PART FOUR

## The Ardennes
## December 1944

# One

On Monday December 5, two days after Shaw's battalion had left Versailles, odd intelligence reports began piling up on desks all across Eisenhower's headquarters. Most were from the British Royal Navy and they consisted of numerous intercepted requests from the German U-Boat High Command for weather reports.

In itself, this was not unusual. Allied planes had long since knocked out most German weather ships, so submarines in the North Atlantic had for some months been sending weather signals back to Berlin. But the sheer number of requests *was* unusual. Odder still, as far as the Allied code breakers could tell, Berlin was asking for predictions only of *bad* weather, not good, particularly later in the month.

Other curious reports began to circulate as well. In England, secret recordings of German POWs turned up a conversation between German officers boasting about a huge offensive scheduled on the western front. It was to begin sometime before Christmas and to involve an astonishing—and in the American view, impossible—forty-six divisions, all gathered along the Rhine across from the Ardennes region of southeast Belgium. Sheer German bluster, the Allies concluded, prisoners trying to bolster their spirits. Meanwhile, a suspicious radio signal picked up in an area of the Ardennes known as the Schnee Eifel apparently called for volunteers who spoke idiomatic American English. But then an abrupt radio silence made it impossible to know what they were to volunteer for.

In Versailles only General Eberhardt was bothered by the radio silence, but he was too discouraged to bring it up in staff meetings. The universal assumption was that the Germans were girding up for battle on the *eastern* front, where they expected a fresh Russian winter advance. There was no reason whatsoever to think the Ardennes were a serious target.

Still, the intelligence units wanted to be thorough. The Ardennes front was General Omar Bradley's responsibility, and in September Bradley had actually discussed the possibility of a German counter-offensive there, after the Allies took Aachen and the Hürtgen Forest to the north of the Ardennes. But in early December he decided that, if anything happened at all, it would be a matter of some four or five divisions at most, a spoiling attack. With the entire Russian army ready to break out of Poland, Hitler would have no time for Belgium, though as Eberhardt liked to point out, the Ardennes was where the Little Corporal Hitler had fought in the First War, and where the Germans had invaded in 1940 and also in the Franco-Prussian War of 1870. It was a route west they knew well. No, Bradley thought, and dismissed his staff. Things were so quiet in the Ardennes, he said in a much-quoted speech, that they might as well call it a "Ghost Front."

On December 3, the day Shaw's unit arrived in the little town of Mourmelon-le-Grand, thirty miles south of the Belgian border, Bradley had roughly 85,000 soldiers in position along the eighty-mile-long front of the Ardennes. He was unaware of the fact that, on the other side of the Our River, hidden by dense forest and nearly complete radio silence, the German army had secretly positioned 200,000 men, with tens of thousands more in reserve.

That same day, in the American rest camp in Bastogne, the glamorous singer Marlene Dietrich, a marvel of sequins and slink, put on three shows for the GIs. She then moved south to Luxembourg City, where she was believed to have spent a *nuit d'amour* with General Patton, or so Patton's adoring soldiers liked to think.

In Paris, meanwhile, Ernest Hemingway had decided to return to the front, but not before he was fully recovered from his bout of pneumonia. In anticipation of action, he bought two white fleece winter jackets, a Thompson submachine gun, a .45 pistol, and box of grenades. Then he went back to the Ritz bar.

Out in the North Atlantic, German submarines continued to study the weather. On December 9 all reports agreed. A cold front of great severity was moving toward Europe and would arrive soon. After it arrived, the region of the Ardennes could expect two weeks of rain, fog, and heavy snow. It was, the submarine commanders were surprised to learn, exactly what the Reich wanted to hear.

The bad weather would begin, said the reports with Teutonic precision, in the early morning of Saturday, December 16.

ACCORDING TO SHAW'S MAP OF FRANCE, A SPECIAL VERSION printed up for the army by the Michelin Tire Company, the village of Mourmelon-le-Grand sat some hundred miles northeast of Paris, in the department of the Marne. Its main tourist attractions, the map added in a sidebar, were the tiled bell tower of the church of St. Lawrence and an ossuary containing the remains of French soldiers killed in the nearby battle of Verdun in 1916.

But soldiers had been living and fighting here long before the battle of Verdun. If Shaw remembered his Roman history, Julius

Caesar had campaigned in the Marne against the Gauls. The present camp had been built in 1857, by order of Emperor Napoleon III, according to a faded sign over the barracks door, and had been in continuous use since the Franco-Prussian War.

"1857," Nagle said. He made a show of sniffing the barracks air and grimacing. "And nobody's fucking cleaned it since."

Nagle was from eastern Connecticut, a former high school wrestling coach. And since every infantry platoon quickly breaks down into preordained, stereotyped roles—hard-assed sergeant, rebel, whiner, showboat, clown—Nagle had somehow devolved into Second Platoon's intellectual. "That's from the Second Empire of France, Captain," he added, "1857."

Shaw was too distracted to do more than nod. They had arrived at the camp in the dark, after midnight, with hooded headlights only on every third truck, so when they piled into their barracks nobody had been able to see anything but stucco walls and concrete floors. Now he was getting a good and thoroughly depressing look.

It was December 4, cold, damp, cloudy. Fog hung in the trees. Fog lay on the ground between buildings, shivering in the cold. A morning to poke your head out, then crawl back under the blankets. As best Shaw could determine, Napoleon III's witless architects had decided that the camp, located in the greenest part of France, should resemble a desert outpost of the Foreign Legion. The stucco, he could now see in the daylight, was painted sandy yellow, the doors had vaguely Moorish arches, the roofs had notched crenellations like a Saharan fort. If a camel had suddenly strolled out of the fog, Shaw wouldn't have been surprised.

Nagle was taking notes for a formal complaint, because Shaw thought his men deserved much better than this—inside there was only one tiny coal-burning stove for each building, next to the single latrine, which (Nagle was right) had probably never been cleaned. The wooden bunks had been hammered together in another century, the mattresses were burlap sacks filled with local straw and thistle. In the middle of the night one of the rickety bunks had simply collapsed, dumping the trooper onto the concrete floor.

"How's Driskell?"

Nagle was busy with his clipboard and didn't answer for a moment. Shaw wondered if the Germans had as many clipboards as the United States Army. Why didn't they just throw clipboards at each other instead of bullets?

"Driskell," Nagle said with studied casualness, "is pantophobic."

Shaw looked up from the drainage pipes he had knelt to examine. "Pantophobic?"

"It means he's scared of everything, Captain. Every little noise. Comes from 'panto,' *all*."

"What do you think?"

"I think he's about ready to shoot himself in the foot and get the hell out of here."

Shaw nodded again. Other battalions of the 101st had already been at Mourmelon-le-Grand for three weeks, waiting to go back into combat. For some people that was a stress worse than being at the front. Desertions were on the rise. He knew that a paratrooper in another battalion had committed suicide with a pistol shot right through the mouth. The ultimate, definitive desertion—"pantomort," as Nagle might say.

"His buddy says he keeps a white handkerchief in his pocket, in case he wants to surrender."

Nagle pulled a slip of green flimsy from the bottom of his clipboard. "Almost forgot, sir. You can make your civilian call to Paris today, 1600 hours." He made another show of squinting to read it. "Annabella March, Hôtel Scribe." He looked up with a gap-toothed grin. "Whaddaya know, Captain Harvard's got a girl."

THE OFFICIAL NAME OF THE LITTLE CAR WAS GENERAL PURPOSE Vehicle, or GPV, universally shortened to "Jeep," the best-loved piece of equipment in the army.

The one B.T. Adams was driving had paper-thin brakes and the temperament of a skittish pony, but Adams had learned to drive on the hard clay, multi-potholed roads of rural Missouri, so the thin brakes and the lumpy unpaved roads of eastern Belgium bothered him not at all. It was the snow that bothered him, the snow and the wind and the constant yakking of the G-2 lieutenant in the shotgun seat, who was by protocol supposed to be driving, but Adams had pulled rank because he liked to be behind the wheel of almost anything.

"You know," the lieutenant said, "most of the Krauts we capture can't drive."

Adams was rising a little in his seat to peer over the windshield. This part of Belgium was as bleak and rugged as he'd been told, and he was losing the road signs under the snow.

"They don't have cars at home like we do," the lieutenant said, "and of course half the German army is pulled around by horses. So the first thing they do with American POWs is make them drive. That's the River Salm over there. You take the next right for St. Vith."

St. Vith was the destination General Eberhardt had picked out for him. Barely six hours after Shaw's 101st rolled out of Versailles, Eberhardt had called Adams in and handed him orders to fly to a British airfield just outside Namur, Belgium. From there he was to proceed to the town of St. Vith and interrogate six new German prisoners whose stories had gotten under his skin. Of course, Eberhardt being Eberhardt, he had held up Adams's departure half an hour in order to tell him, first that St. Vith was named after St. Vitus, he of the herky-jerky dance, and second to recite the history of Namur, including the completely irrelevant fact that the great seventeenth-century French military engineer Vauban had once built an impregnable citadel there (quickly leveled, he added cheerfully, by the unimpressed Austrians).

They pulled into St. Vith just after noon, an ugly clutter of intersecting roads and depressing, widely scattered stone buildings. To the east of the town rose a dark forested ridge called the Schnee Eifel—"schnee" meant "snow," the lieutenant told him, "eifel" was just the local name for the ridge. At the western end, just above St. Vith, a five-mile wide valley called the Losheim Gap cut straight across the ridge from Germany to Belgium like a pipeline. This was the corridor that invading German armies had swarmed through in 1870, 1914, and 1940, the danger point that Eberhardt had rapped again and again on his maps. Defending it were approximately eight hundred American troops, mostly untested replacements scattered in foxholes they called "sugar bowls" up and down the Schnee. Some ten or fifteen miles to the east, if you believed the rumors, half the German army sat poised to attack.

"Welcome to the Ghost Front," the lieutenant said as they pulled up to his headquarters, "where the living is easy."

Headquarters here was yet another schoolhouse, this one gray-stoned, charmless, and sweating ice on the outside, but surprisingly comfortable inside. The 106th Infantry Division had commandeered the ground floor, with its two pot-bellied stoves and a fine slate-lined fireplace in the principal's office. At least a dozen officers and enlisted men milled around the coals, doing, as far as Adams could see, nothing at all but drinking coffee.

One flight up was G-2, Division Intelligence, ten or twelve men and twice that many desks in a former classroom that overlooked the town square. Like the town, the square was a bare, sullen, mostly empty space the color of cold ashes. Adams rubbed condensation off a window. No fountain or monument under the snow, no decorations, no flags, no benches. The few shops he could see had nothing in their windows. All the signs were in German.

"Because," the lieutenant said, "this godforsaken place used to be in Germany, back before 1940. Most of the people think they're German, not Belgian. That's your desk, sir, and that stack of imperishable prose is all our reports for the past two weeks, just like the general ordered. You can interview the prisoners right away, or flip through those first, whichever."

Although it was warm in the room, the lieutenant pulled up his collar and hugged himself. He was from Florida, he had told Adams. He glared at the window, where snow was beginning to patter against the glass. "Twenty-five degrees out there. Must be nice in Paris, sir."

Without thinking, Adams found himself repeating one of Shaw's silly sayings. "I cannot approve of our climate."

The lieutenant turned around, puzzled.

Where the hell did that come from? Adams's thoughts suddenly scattered like marbles—Shaw, Annie March, General Eberhardt and his discontents, a town where everybody spoke German. He scraped back a chair and sat down at the desk. "Reports first," he said.

It took no more than half an hour for Adams to begin to share Eberhardt's worries. The first batch of reports came from a traffic analysis platoon of the 114th Signal Corps, which was monitoring German radio communications along a ten-mile stretch of the Schnee Eifel. Despite the general radio silence, from time to time uncoded blasts had been detected, usually clear text messages without any punctuation or adjectives, just verbs, nouns, and numbers. Individually, they made little sense. Collectively, they suggested…

what? Adams scribbled numbers and waited to see them fall into a pattern, because sooner or later numbers always did. But these didn't. He looked again at the distribution headers.

"Your colonel didn't send these forward to Versailles," he said to the lieutenant.

"No, sir."

"Why not?"

The lieutenant shrugged. "Didn't want to rock the boat, I guess."

Bored and cold, the Florida lieutenant turned on Radio Luxembourg and Adams put aside the traffic analysis papers to sift through what the army called S-3 (Operations) logs for the area. To the background of "Don't Fence Me In" by the Andrews Sisters, he flipped page after page until he came to an entry that would have had Eberhardt jumping up and down: *Two strange officers reported to the Armored Field Battalion asking about communication systems and artillery placement. Descriptions: A captain wearing .45 cal. pistol, height 6 foot, 1 inch, about 210 lbs. Dressed in a new trench coat. A 1st Lieutenant with carbine, new trench coat and uniform. About 5 foot ten, 175 lbs.*

"This wasn't forwarded either."

The lieutenant was drumming his fingers in time to the music. "We get a lot of visitors, sir."

There was more—near the town of Malmedy a jeep was stopped because it was carrying four people and army jeeps never carried more than three. When the driver tried to get away, the MPs opened fire and killed all four, who turned out to be German infiltrators in American Third Army uniforms. Another German, also in an American uniform, was killed when he tried to buy cigarettes with US dollars, a bad mistake because American soldiers were paid in specially printed military scrip and didn't use dollars.

At four o'clock Adams sat in on an interrogation of two new German prisoners. A native German speaker from Wisconsin was in charge, a Sergeant Klippel, who was red-faced and impatient and liked to jab his finger as he talked. The interview, as they were required to call it, had been going on for an hour when Adams slipped into the room, and Klippel had reached the point where he was leaning over the German, a kid of eighteen or nineteen, and yelling. He glanced over at Adams, then poked the German in the chest.

"Last time," he said in ugly German. "What unit?"

Some of the younger prisoners cried under this kind of bullying. This one smirked. "Sixth Panzer Army, General Josef Dietrich. Roosevelt is a pig."

Klippel slapped him hard.

The kid blinked but said nothing. Klippel looked at Adams. "He's lying. The fucking Sixth Panzer is in Poland, sir. We know that for a fact." He slapped the German one more time and told the guard to get him out of there.

The other prisoner was a *Volksgrenadier* who asked for Lucky Strike cigarettes and said he belonged to an engineering unit that specialized in bridging rivers. Adams sat down beside him and despite Klippel's disapproving glare shook open a pack of Luckies. "What's a bridge building unit doing here?"

The German shook his head, a man who just took orders and didn't ask why. He was big and husky and stupid, a welder by trade before the war. He had applied to a Waffen-SS *Junkerschule* when he enlisted, an officer candidate school for "young nobles," but flunked out. Now he built bridges, he said, strong ones; strong enough to carry Tiger tanks across a river.

Adams was tired, uneasy. A Tiger tank could weigh seventy-five tons. A Tiger tank only belonged to elite panzer units. A Tiger tank had no business being on the Ghost Front. His thoughts scattered again and jumped from tanks and bridges to Annie March and Annie March's sentence about bridges and Annie March walking away from him in the Hôtel Scribe. He missed Shaw. He thought of Shaw in combat, bullets flying toward him, Annie March flying toward him.

"A lot of bridges in the Ardennes," the German said smugly. "You'll see in about a week."

# Two

THE 333RD FIELD ARTILLERY BATTALION WAS AN AFRICAN-AMER-ican unit, one of the few all-black combat units in Europe. It had landed in Normandy in July and seen fierce, continuous front-line action since then. Its senior officers were white, as regulations required. Its enlisted men were not allowed in white mess halls and canteens. They *were* allowed to give blood, but not to white men. Its wounded—and there were many—could only be treated in black hospital wards. When they entered a military base, the bus or truck had to stop at the gate so that the blacks could exit and walk in. At USO shows, black soldiers sat behind German POWs, in segregated sections. When they met, black soldiers had a secret fraternal sign, a double V with both hands, to signify "Victory on Two Fronts." The second front was the US Army.

Annie March knew all this because British *Vogue,* after reject-ing her article on black nurses, had undergone a change of heart and asked if she had any ideas for a story about black *soldiers.*

And so the day after Shaw's Company D left Versailles, try-ing to find something to do, she had gone back to her nurses. They were sympathetic, if wary, but not much help. They knew nothing at all about deployments and assignments. Though they sometimes received letters and calls from boyfriends, army censorship concealed locations. They had no idea where she might go to find the 333rd or any other black battalion, for that matter. Black soldiers, they said, might as well be invisible. Weary, they turned back to their patients.

Annie spent the next day on the phone and then a full afternoon at B.T. Adams's Versailles unit, but B.T. wasn't there and nobody would talk to her except B.T.'s garrulous commanding officer, who had once read an article on Thomas Jefferson that her father had written. Feet on his desk, cigar in his mouth, he spun out a long monologue on Jefferson's many black mistresses and mulatto children. He was from Arkansas, he explained, and knew about Negroes.

It was Martha to the rescue, naturally. Like the sorceress she was, on the third day Martha listened quietly to Annie's complaints, then excused herself to go upstairs to her room in the Scribe. She came back ten minutes later with a brand new copy of *Yank* magazine whose last page featured a picture of the 333rd, though it said nothing about its present location.

Annie flipped through the magazine, admired its photographs and deplored its prose, which was even duller, she thought than her own. "No help here," she said and handed back the magazine.

Martha excused herself again and was gone for twenty minutes. When she came back she sat down, swallowed some of her magic potion of scotch and lemon juice, and put two telephone memo slips on the table. On the first she had scribbled in her gnomic handwriting "333rd" and the name of a town in Belgium. Bastogne.

The second slip said simply Mourmelon-le-Grand.

"Which latter," she said, "now hosteth temporarily the First Battalion, 101st Airborne, Company D, keep your panties on, you're welcome. Now we're even."

"Maybe." Annie read the slips twice over and folded them into her shirt pocket. "Did you call Hemingway for these?"

Martha's lovely oval-shaped face grew longer, tighter, mask-like, a preview of age to come. "No," she said, "not ever."

Later, curious, Annie asked the Scribe receptionist, whose English was good and nosiness extreme. Madame Gellhorn had called General James Gavin, the receptionist said, commander of the 82nd Airborne, and was put ight through.

ADAMS STAYED FOUR NIGHTS IN THE NEAREST PLACE HE COULD find a bunk. This was in a house some twelve or thirteen miles east of St. Vith, on the outskirts of a drab village called Manderfeld, which had a small executive command post manned by the 14th Cavalry. He requisitioned a jeep and drove there himself.

The house belonged to a German-speaking blacksmith, who greeted his unwanted guest with a sneer and a terse speech about American tyrants. It was not the German he had learned at Harvard, and the house had nothing like the comfort of the Hôtel de la Reine in Versailles. The blacksmith gave him his teenage son's room and a wool blanket—the son slept in the barn—but little else except repeated hostile glowers. Adams had brought a can of coffee from the 106th and asked the wife to make him coffee in the morning to go with the baguette and butter that served as breakfast. He would have shared it with the blacksmith, but by the time Adams woke at six the blacksmith had already gone off to work, not to return until nightfall.

"Must be a lot of horses here," he said the second morning. The son Hasso was feeding their two pigs and said nothing.

"My grandfather had a farm," Adams said, "just outside St. Louis. He plowed with mules."

"St. Louis," the boy grinned. "Chicago. New York." He was short and stocky with big wrists and hands, a blacksmith's son, and even though the temperature was well below freezing and snow covered the ground, he wore only a thin cotton jacket and a stocking cap.

"Thing is," Adams said, "I don't see so many farms around here, just logging trails and hardscrabble." He couldn't figure out how to say "hardscrabble" in German, so fell back on "just logging trails and rocks."

Hasso finished throwing pig slop into the pen and they both stood in cold, companionable silence, watching a wrinkling pink snout inch out of the sty. Adams offered a sip of his coffee, but the kid shook his head and looked, without much subtlety, at the pack of cigarettes in Adams's jacket pocket. Adams didn't smoke, but cigarettes were universal currency and he carried his ration of them everywhere. He shook a couple out.

"So where does your father go every morning, if there's not much work here?"

The boy pointed east toward the Losheim Gap. "There's business there."

Adams thought of the yakking lieutenant's remark about German soldiers not driving, using horses to pull artillery.

"But you don't help him?"

The boy grinned again. "I'm helping him," he said. "I'm watching you."

Adams finished going over the Interrogation reports by noon and decided that, while it was still light and for once not snowing, he would get a little closer to the Schnee Eifel and see for himself what kind of terrain a German attack would have to pass through.

His lieutenant wasn't available, but Sergeant Klippel was, and by one o'clock Adams was back in his jeep, passenger side this time, climbing what he automatically calculated was a six-degree grade up a logging road, into a dark Germanic forest.

Adams knew little about trees, just enough to recognize beeches, spruce, and oak. Even these he found hard to distinguish as the dense forest crowded in and the afternoon brightness, such as it was, began to fall from the air. They passed through a line of lightly manned foxholes, gave the password, and pushed higher. Around two o'clock the jeep bounced and jolted to a halt at what the map said was the crest of the Eifel ridge, some 700 meters above St. Vith and its valley, twelve miles from the German border.

What the map didn't show was the darkness of the woods. Or the stillness of the trees. Or the utter silence when Klippel turned off the motor. Adams climbed out of the jeep and started over the snow to an outcropping of slate that looked as though it might give him a view eastward toward the Rhine. After a dozen steps he remembered Shaw's lecture about German forests and wolves and witches, and he shivered and turned back for the carbine that Klippel kept in the jeep. There wouldn't be any wolves. There might be Nazi patrols.

"See that?" Klippel materialized beside him, also carrying a carbine.

On the other side of the slate outcropping the road cut sharply downhill. Here, its ruts were new tire treads and freshly churned mud. Off to one side the snow had been walked over by so many shoes that a carpet of icy black leaves showed through. Some twenty yards past the road a shadow lay curled on the snow, a still life composition in black on white, except for a crust of reddish brown where a bullet had passed through the skull.

Klippel crept forward and turned the body over. A civilian in his fifties, shot twice in the back of his head.

The forest wasn't so quiet, after all, Adams thought. He could hear his pulse drumming. He could hear his breath sawing. Klippel darted a few feet past him, half-crouched, rifle cradled in his gloves, eyes wary, and Adams remembered another of Shaw's ideas, that every American boy, even if he grew up in the Bronx, thought he could stalk through the woods like Daniel Boone.

"Could have been Krauts," Klippel said. "Or one of his friendly neighbors. Plenty of blood feuds around here. Somebody collaborates. Somebody else takes care of him. You ready to go back, sir? It's all like this, just woods."

There had been a subtle change in Adams's pulse. The drumming sound was now a low growl, like a motor. The air stirred uneasily.

"That's too fucking close." Klippel sprinted toward the jeep and Adams, on his heels, clambered in just as the tires started to spin. Klippel tap danced on the brakes and the clutch and a German half-track burst over the ridge, out of the trees, like a breaching gray whale.

They were a hundred yards down the logging road when Klippel slowed for a curve and the first shots raked the trees overhead. Somehow, as the steering wheel bucked and jumped in his hands, Klippel passed Adams a rifle. He turned and sighted, and the driver of the half-track appeared by magic on the end of the barrel, which he knew from training snipers called "the beauty spot."

With the incredible velocity of thought Adams realized that he had never been in actual combat before, that Shaw had faced live bullets over and over, while he pored over maps and numbers or handed out cigarettes to teenage kids. A badly flawed part of himself, an envious, insecure part of himself that he hated, suddenly asked if he were as brave as Shaw, as good as Shaw, a soldier like Shaw.

His finger wrapped around the trigger. The half-track kept coming. Now he could see faces clearly. A soldier behind the half-track's mounted machine gun fired again, but too high, and cascading bark and snow blinded them for a moment. Klippel stomped the brakes for another switchback. From what seemed a long way off Adams heard the whirr and cough of the jeep's motor as it tried not to stall. For an impossibly long second the jeep sat sideways on the road. The world went motionless.

"Shoot the fucker!"

Adams hesitated. The machine gunner had black hair creeping out of his helmet. Weren't Germans usually blonde? Adams thought. Odd. The rifle sight rose on its own, like the prow of a boat on a wave. Adams held his breath and waited till it came down again and then squeezed the trigger and because he was a mathematician counted the shots, did the numbers, watched as the bright copper shells flew out of the breech in a tumbling arc. Then the world began to move again, and Klippel had them through a clearing, bouncing and skidding their way toward St. Vith. The half-track clattered to a halt far behind them.

When he looked over, Klippel was nodding and holding one thumb up.

"I didn't think you were going to fucking shoot, sir, pardon my language."

"I'm not sure if I hit anybody."

Klippel grinned. "Doesn't matter, sir. Desk soldier like you— that was fucking righteous!"

# Three

"It's like living in the *Iliad*," Shaw said. "Thousands and thousands of stories, everybody has a different war. There's going to be no end of books."

"My father used to say a man went to war in the *Iliad* and came home in the *Odyssey*," Annie said.

Shaw smiled. "It's hard to compete with your father."

Annie blushed and looked down. "You're not the first boy to say that."

She folded and refolded the napkin beside her glass. Some "boy." Captain John Michael Shaw was wearing a bulky canvas army jacket, muddy pants and boots, and a permanent look of pain in his eyes that was years away from being a "boy." *When did you cross the line?* she wondered. She met someone by purest accident, a guy, a soldier, just another soldier like all the men around her, all the men crowding her, flirting with her, grabbing her—*how did you choose him?* But she had. At some point, as effortlessly as taking her next breath, she had chosen this one and he had simply taken his place in her life.

It was eight–fifteen in the evening, Thursday, December 14, and they were sitting in the plain ground-floor restaurant of the

Hôtel Alfa, pride of Luxembourg City. The Hôtel Alfa was also the headquarters of General Omar Bradley's First Army Group, so it was no real surprise that before Shaw could say anything a ruckus began at the door—a springing of soldiers to their feet, a stentorian chorus of "Tenn-hutts!" and then Omar Bradley himself ambled into the room.

Shaw came to attention like all the other men. Annie hesitated, not sure what a non-soldier woman reporter should do, then compromised by half rising from her chair. Bradley walked toward them on his way to his table by the window, nodding, waving a genial salute. He frowned at Shaw's muddy uniform but kept walking, and Annie saw an unprepossessing man about fifty, with thinning hair and protruding ears. He said something to an orderly in a high-pitched voice, and Annie struggled for a moment to identify his accent.

"He's from Missouri," Shaw said, reading her mind, as she was finding lovers do. "Like B.T."

Neither of them had mentioned B.T. so far. Annie began to look down at the table again, then decided that when you fall in love you should say so.

"I didn't see B.T. in Paris, not alone anyway. I didn't want to."

"He's—"

Annie popped to her feet, flipped an impertinent salute to the back of Omar Bradley's balding head, and said, "I came all this way through sleet and snow and dead of night to see Luxembourg City." She pulled him to his feet. "With my boyfriend."

Outside it was cold, bitter bone-snapping cold. All her life Annie would remember how cold it was in Europe in the winter of 1944. As a practical matter, she was dressed more or less like Shaw—thick army jacket, army boots, shapeless six-button-fly khaki trousers and a watch cap pulled over her ears. But she hadn't spent two months in Paris for nothing. Instead of something wool and practical around her neck, she wore a blue and white silk scarf that she had bought at the Givenchy perfume store on the rue de Rivoli. The scarf was wispy and feminine and decorated with little golden perfume flacons around the borders, which somehow delighted her. Despite the cold she could still smell perfume. She hoped that Shaw could too and that it was driving him crazy.

"That's an awful place," Shaw said, and they both turned to look at the seven-story brick box that was the Hôtel Alfa. "Must have been a German architect."

"Tell me about Mourmelon-le-Grand," Annie said, taking his arm contentedly. "Martha kept calling it 'Watermelon-le-Grand' and saying you had already suffered enough for your country."

"It's not grand," Shaw conceded. He lifted her arm gently and put his own arm around her waist to draw her closer. "But it has a church with a tiled steeple."

"We must look like two of those puffy tire men you see on the Michelin maps, especially with my glasses."

Shaw pulled her closer, put one finger on her cheek—*it's cold,* she thought, *it doesn't matter,* she thought—and kissed her softly. "Nobody cares what we look like."

Luxembourg City sat on a three-hundred-foot-deep gorge, carved long ago into a plateau of soft sandstone by the convergence of two rivers, the Alzette and the Pétrusse. The upper section of the city was crisscrossed by what seemed to Annie like dozens of ugly modern bridges. The lower part, the Ville Basse, lay along the banks of the Alzette, a charming medieval maze of alleys, little squares, and stone buildings that had lost their upright posture and begun to tilt and nod over the tiny streets. Armies naturally preferred the open, defensible upper section, where the ubiquitous Vauban had constructed a fort. Lovers preferred the Ville Basse.

It was pitch dark now everywhere, except down beside the Alzette, where a few ancient, creaking taverns had old-fashioned gas lanterns outside their doors. They paused to look at the flashes of running water, living streaks of white and yellow hurrying past. In what was doubtless some primordial soldierly impulse Shaw knelt and waved his hand in the current for a moment, as if measuring something.

Overhead on one of the bridges a tank rumbled eastward, grinding up the silence. When it had passed, they heard the faint plink of a piano coming from the nearest tavern, and Shaw with his familiar kid grin took her hand and they both stooped through a very old, very low door and walked in.

What Annie hadn't expected was the sweet calmness of everything. They had been exchanging notes, calls, messages of every kind for the last eight days—Shaw had called in every favor known to man, he said, to wrangle a two-day leave from Mourmelon. Annie had pestered the First Army motor pool in Bastogne every day until a weary corporal promised her a lift to Luxembourg. They were lovers and they were going to be lovers and everything should have been feverish and hurried and on fire—bodices ripped, buttons flying—and instead here they were, in some walled off space of quiet and trust that was not better than what was to come, but somehow… She searched for a word. Bigger. Safer.

The owner of the tavern was a talker, fat and Falstaffian. Without being asked, he brought them a bottle of greenish Alsatian wine, poured two glasses, and in a pleasant but guttural French told them his wife would bring them a winter beef stew that was made of real beef, the good kind they had hidden from the Germans during the Occupation. Then he sat down with them, poured himself a glass of wine, and began to tell them what the Occupation had been like—how nobody was allowed to speak

French, how the street names were changed to German, the young males conscripted into the German army. All the Jews had to wear gold stars, he said, until, a dozen or so at a time, they all disappeared. "October 19, 1941," he said solemnly, "Luxembourg was officially declared '*Judenrein*.'"

Annie looked a question.

"Cleansed of Jews."

There were a few other people in the tavern, regulars, busy with their food, not interested in yet another Yank with a girl. Annie didn't want to think about *Judenrein* or the war. She turned her mind toward the piano player in the corner, a dark-haired, long-faced woman playing American songs, quite badly. Annie recognized "Boogie Woogie Bugle Boy of Company B" and "Don't Sit Under the Apple Tree," but then sat back and tuned her out because the owner's wife had arrived with the stew and another bottle of wine.

As she ladled and poured, the tavern owner finally stood up to leave. But first he reached over and rubbed his fingers across the captain's bars on Shaw's jacket.

"Your man here, he's a good soldier?"

Annie looked at Shaw and had no idea what to say.

"I ask because a good soldier has to *hate* till he burns with it. I see him here with a pretty girl—a pretty girl who speaks very good French—and I say, I wonder if he hates enough?"

"Bruno." The wife began to tug him away.

"I like them," Bruno said. "He's a liberator." He leaned over and whispered confidentially in Shaw's ear, then stepped back, patted his big belly, couldn't help himself and grinned at Annie. "I told him there's a room upstairs, if you want it."

"*Bruno!*" his wife cried, but she smiled all the same.

By eleven the little tavern was almost empty and the piano player had long departed. Annie had no idea really of what they had been talking about—cameras, Boston, Harvard professors, the mystery of Martha and General Gavin. For whatever reason her eyes strayed again to the piano, and John Michael—she was going to have to decide what to call him—was he the kind of man who needed two names? She didn't know. Abruptly, John Michael stood up and led her to the piano, where for a minute or two he played the Mozart she remembered from the first night they had met in Paris. Suddenly grinning like Bruno, he drew her down to the bench, on his right, and put her right hand on the keyboard.

"I can't play. My mother made me take lessons for a month, but I was so awful about it—"

He placed his hand on hers, lightly, and began to press. His fingers moved her fingers, the keys obeyed, notes floated into air, evanescent as snowflakes, fading into the chilly air, and she found they were playing "I Dream of Jeanie with the Light Brown Hair," so American and beautiful that her eyes filled with tears. Softly, John or Michael or Shaw began to sing, but with "Annie" in the song, not "Jeanie," and there were still tears in her eyes when he closed the piano and led her up the stairs, because they had chosen each other.

# Four

On that same day, Thursday, December 14, his driver sick with flu, B.T. Adams drove himself from St. Vith to the considerably larger market town of Bastogne, some eighty kilometers to the southwest.

Like Luxembourg City, Bastogne had been liberated in September, but then the advancing wave of Americans had stalled and, in a literal sense, lost energy—their fuel supply lines from France were now so long and stretched so thin that until the logistics of managing eight hundred thousand men could be worked out, nobody was going anywhere.

He entered the town through a massive stone gate called the porte de Trèves, which his Michelin map informed him was part of a defensive wall, built by somebody called John the Blind in the 14th century, but mostly in ruins now. He circled through narrow streets that looked like those in any other French or Belgian town he'd seen so far—a terrible place to maneuver tanks and half-tracks, he automatically thought, being military now, being Eberhardt's protégé now. Then his mind circled back—*Built in the 14th century! The goddamned 14th century!* Armies had been raking blood and bones back and forth over this gloomy patch of land for *six hundred years*, and weren't done yet. By definition, man is a social animal, Shaw used to say drily, quoting Aristotle.

The headquarters of the VIII Corps Cavalry Group was in the Hôtel de Ville, an unimpressive nineteenth-century limestone pile, on the inevitable town square with the inevitable fountain and wasp-waisted statue of a soldier from the 1914 war. Inside he found the G-2 offices and had a coded report wired to Eberhardt at Versailles. And then…then he was at a loose end.

His orders were to wait at Bastogne until Eberhardt replied. If the general wanted him back in Paris, Bastogne had an airfield. If he wanted him to stay in Belgium, it would probably be to drive back to the Schnee Eifel and look around again. Meanwhile, a pair of S-3 captains invited him to dinner at a Negro artillery regiment on the outskirts of Bastogne—the 333rd they said, the best food you ever had. But over the past few months Adams had become more rigid, more soldierly, as he thought of it. His orders were to wait at headquarters, which was what he would do. He liked the clarity of orders. He took a quick meal in the officers' mess and settled down in the anteroom/bar next to the communications room.

A dreary evening, nothing about it to make you think you were in a war. Outside, snow flurries mixed improbably with fog, the temperature fell to the twenties. Inside, the anteroom was taken over by gossiping officers listening to the radio and talking about movies. When the news came on, they learned that Eisenhower had been promoted to five stars and was attending his valet's wedding. The bandleader Glenn Miller had disappeared in a plane bound from London to Paris. The weather in eastern Belgium looked to continue cold and foggy. A British colonel asked why Adams was in Bastogne instead of Paris, then repeated Bradley's line about the Ghost Front and told him he was wasting his time. Go look outside at the sky. Not even Germans would fight in weather like that.

At eleven his reply from Versailles came through. Stay in Bastogne. Wait for orders. He drank three snifters of sour brandy and thought about Paris and Annabella March and went off to find a bed.

He woke at five-thirty, in the dark, feeling the same nervous drumming in his pulse as he had felt up on the Schnee Eifel. A cook was fooling around in the enlisted men's mess tent, making porridge. He gave Adams a mug of coffee and Adams walked out into the nearest street and stood in the cold wet air and watched pinpoints of light moving about in the headquarters windows. Every American boy could stalk silently through the woods like Daniel Boone. Every American boy could sense when trouble was building up, out in the darkness.

Bastogne was technically a forward combat site, but nobody seemed to take that seriously. The German Air Force was a joke. Blackout was a joke. Already bright lights were showing in the windows, soldiers were stirring.

An infantry platoon assembled down the street, muffled voices, cigarette embers. Truck lights pointed them toward the porte de Trèves, and a raw-voiced sergeant barked them into formation. Adams followed the platoon as it started off on its patrol, but veered away at the gate, took out his flashlight, and climbed slick, mossy steps to the top of John the Blind's wall. From there he could still see nothing but darkness, but he could feel a cold wind coming off the mountains to the east, the Ardennes, and he could feel his pulse drumming faster and faster, and he didn't know why.

It was an uncertainty that bothered him. As a person, Adams would have said, he was reasonably well-balanced. His highs were not too high, his lows were not too low. The rush of adrenaline on the Schnee Eifel when they were chased by the half-track had been uncharacteristic—a moment, an episode—and even then he had kept his cool, counting shells, squeezing the trigger like a veteran.

As always, his mind went back to Shaw. Shaw's highs went much higher, his lows much lower. Shaw in full battle fury, he thought, Shaw when his feelings were at their furious, blood-bursting height, Shaw must be something to see—the very incarnation of *rage militaire*. And Shaw on the other hand, Shaw after his soldier Wilcox was killed in Holland—Shaw when his feelings plunged—that was rage that blew through everything and then turned to paralysis, visible pain.

Shaw's highs were so much higher than his own, Adams thought, because he empathized with other people. Not with numbers. And Shaw's lows were so much lower than his own because…here Adams's mind slowed and came to a halt. Because Shaw was greatly capable of love.

The wind picked up, bringing news of the east. Snow lifted from the ground and swirled a few steps forward. If you squinted hard enough, Adams imagined, you could almost see the first distant stabs of light beyond the mountains that would mean dawn was at hand.

At eleven-thirty that morning word finally came from Versailles. Eberhardt had just received the strange, very strange report that more than two hundred military searchlights had been loaded onto German trains at Koblenz. The likeliest destination, the report guessed, was the town of Prüm, just east of the Losheim Gap, but this was information gleaned from informants inside the Reich, not necessarily reliable. Still, Eberhardt thought, still…the Losheim Gap. What did the Germans want with two hundred spotlights at the Losheim Gap?

Sighing, Adams climbed back in his jeep and began the weary drive back to St. Vith.

As he drove, he let his mind drift, thinking at times about his last paper in graduate school—on a problem in topological algebra, something called "countable tightness in a *k*-space"—at other times about Eberhardt and Eberhardt's unending worries, a countable tightness if there ever was one.

And yet. The general was no fool. Two hundred searchlights. The strategically placed town of Prüm. Railway informants. Adams's thoughts took another leap.

One of his jobs in Versailles was analyzing German railroad traffic along the western front, a job that called for his particular talent of visualizing number patterns as if they were contoured on a map. And one of the many things he had learned from Eberhardt was the importance of railways in German warfare. Indeed, Adams's first night in Versailles had been given over to an Eberhardtian lecture on trains and the Franco-Prussian War of 1870, when the Germans made a number of costly miscalculations concerning rolling stock and empty troop cars. Germans are smart, Eberhardt had said. After the war, *train scheduling* became a required subject at the Berlin War Academy.

*Conclusion Number One*, Adams thought—*every one of Hitler's staff officers had taken classes in how to draw up an efficient railroad timetable.*

*Conclusion Number Two—if German trains were moving searchlights to the Ardennes, there was a reason. Germans were not inefficient.*

It was snowing again now. In a village, whose name Adams couldn't read, MPs directed him around a closed road and north toward the town of Malmedy, where he would have to turn south again to reach St. Vith. He navigated the last ten miles like John the Blind, groping through fog now, not snow, and at six o'clock finally pulled up in front the schoolhouse headquarters again.

Here he learned that he was still quartered with the same unfriendly German-speaking blacksmith in the distant village of Manderfeld. With a sigh, he gassed up the jeep and headed east again. This time, when he pulled up, the wife barely looked at him, while her husband sat by the stove and smoked a pipe. Once, the son Hasso walked by and his father, uncharacteristically genial, playfully rumpled his hair, then smirked at Adams.

At nine o'clock Adams wrote two letters to Annabella March, both of which he crumpled and tossed away. At one in the morning, pulse drumming again, he woke and pulled aside the curtains in his bedroom. Ankle-deep snow, and above the snow a world of fog and bone-snapping cold. Shaw, he supposed, would have thought about the poor GIs freezing in their foxholes out on the Schnee Eifel. He wasn't Shaw and couldn't be Shaw. He thought about trains and searchlights.

When he woke again it was five o'clock in the morning, Saturday, December 16. Without quite knowing why, he dressed and slipped out the front door into the fog. Nothing in the world was colder than winter fog, he thought, and shivered in his jacket. Aimlessly, he took a few steps over the crusted snow. When he stopped, he saw that he was not the only one awake. There was a light on in the blacksmith's bedroom and the blacksmith himself was standing at the window, looking at the Schnee.

# Five

At fifteen minutes past five that same morning, General Eccard von Manteuffel, commander of the Fifth German Panzer Army, stepped outside a farmhouse just south of Prüm. He was twenty kilometers east of the blacksmith's garden in Manderfeld where Adams was standing.

In Prüm, close to the river, it was even colder than it was in Manderfeld, and the snow ranged from ankle deep to hip deep. Wet rags of fog clung to the trees. But if it was eerily quiet in Manderfeld, around Manteuffel's farmhouse the air was busy with whispers and the scrape of boots. Odd, unidentifiable clicks in the darkness sounded like metallic crickets. Somewhere nearby a horse whinnied and Manteuffel, a former cavalry officer, automatically turned in its direction. Then he walked purposefully down a cleared path and stopped beside an idling Mark IV Panther tank and laid a reassuring hand on its iron flank, as if it were one of his old mounts at the war academy. Manteuffel was only five feet two inches tall—his friends called him *Kleiner* ("Little")—but he projected an astonishing force of personality. Even Hitler was supposed to be in awe of him. A few staffers had followed him down the path, keeping a respectful distance, and now they watched, shadows in the fog, as he lifted his wrist to study his watch.

Along the ridges of the Schnee Eifel, scattered groups of the American 28th Infantry were beginning their usual morning routine, walking out in sleepy groups of two or three to their fox-holes, which had been left empty all night. To the Germans who had been monitoring the Schnee for weeks, it was typical lazy, soft American behavior—after sundown, rather than stay outside in the punishing cold, they took shelter in farmhouses and barns behind the main road along the ridge, nicknamed by some wag the "Sky Line Drive."

One of these Americans was the lieutenant who had first driven Adams to St. Vith, now rotated to the Schnee for routine duty. In the village of Hosingen he climbed up to an observation post in a church steeple, where a yawning corporal had just settled down beside his radio. It was an ideal looking post, high enough to show the faint bluish outline of the River Our through the fog, sheltered enough from the wind to be bearable. The lieu-tenant squinted at his watch. It was exactly 5:30 am. The corporal cupped his hands around a cigarette to light it.

Sometimes when you look directly at a tiny point of light, your eyes multiply it, until for a moment a whole field of flickering white dots covers your retina. A common optical phe-nomenon. The dots disappear quickly. The lieutenant, used to it, looked away from the corporal's cigarette toward the eastern hori-zon. There, just as you would expect, the black sky shimmered with countless pinpoints of light. The lieutenant thought about a cigarette himself. He glanced at the corporal, then for some rea-son back at the horizon. And at that instant the dots turned into lightning flashes and the sky blew apart.

The corporal reached for his radio. The lieutenant stared in awe.

Up and down the Ghost Front, for eighty-five long and frozen miles, German artillery had erupted, blasting away at the Schnee Eifel—mortars up close, rockets farther back on launching platforms, 88 artillery along the river, a Wagnerian maelstrom of fire and thunder. Deep behind the river railroad guns began to sling fourteen-inch shells far over the ridges and into the villages beyond.

The church steeple began to quiver. The fir trees below, like frightened men, shook snow from their limbs. Over the unearthly whine of the Nebelwerfer mortars—"screaming meemies" to the Americans—the corporal tried to radio his company commander that something had happened, but the noise was deafening, nobody could understand him. He dropped his microphone and came to his feet beside the lieutenant. On their left, on their right, as far as they could see, it was as if the sun had suddenly burst out of the ground and turned the air itself to flames. They did not know it yet—no American knew it yet—but the last and greatest battle of the war had begun.

THE ENORMOUS BOMBARDMENT WAS PLANNED TO CONTINUE FOR two full hours, even three hours along the northernmost part of the front. But because Manteuffel had defiantly told Hitler that a long bombardment would interfere with his mobility, at Prüm the artillery barrage was lighter and shorter. Just before six a.m. the little general swung around and snapped an order. Almost at once, up and down his line, two hundred tanks, mostly the big twenty-seven-ton Mark IVs, roared to life and started toward the river and the bridges and the Losheim Gap. Ahead of them, beside them, behind them—on foot and in a wild assortment of trucks, artillery, and armored cars—came the thirty thousand grenadiers of the Fifth Panzer Army Group.

Waiting in their foxholes above the Gap were roughly eight hundred Americans.

In the blacksmith's garden at Manderfeld, slack-jawed, too stunned even to shiver, B.T. Adams stood in the cold watching the fiery ridge of the Schnee. When the first of the railroad shells landed behind him, he turned and dashed to his room for his gear. On the stairs the blacksmith grinned at him and clapped his hands. Outside again, running for the jeep, Adams saw one of the railroad shells—big as an ashcan—sing past overhead and explode in the village.

He stopped and looked east again and suddenly understood the mystery of the searchlights—all along the front the Germans had flicked them on, bouncing their light off the low clouds and onto the snow, creating a strange unworldly artificial moonlight. Had he been closer to the Gap he would have seen Manteuffel's soldiers swarming out of the fog, over a landscape doubly illuminated by the searchlights and the snow, waves of ghostly white-sheeted forms that marched or ran in formation, twelve to fourteen across, toward their river crossings and the wide open path into Belgium.

Adams had little experience—and no patience—with panic. On the ground floor of the St. Vith schoolhouse headquarters he found nothing but chaos—junior officers shouting at each other, overturned desks, staffers frantically destroying papers as the artillery hit closer and closer. In the principal's elegant paneled office, a sergeant was on his knees shoveling cardboard files into the fireplace. Disgusted, Adams pushed his way upstairs to the G-2 rooms.

Here the chaos was confined to the radio operators, who were keeping up a continuous din of orders, counter-orders, and obscenities, because the telephone wires on the Schnee had been destroyed by the barrage and every radio wavelength was playing

German band music. Reflexively, drawn like a magnet, Adams went to the map wall and planted himself in front of the biggest map. Better than screaming voices, the numbers and contoured lines would tell him what was happening.

"They said the Krauts only had two 88s on a horse-drawn carriage!"

Adams ignored whoever had said that.

At the window somebody yelled that he saw German M-2 jet planes, Hitler's new weapon. Adams ignored him too. A hand shook papers in front of his eyes. Adams knocked it away.

What was happening was exactly what Eberhardt had predicted, only here, on the ground, having been to the Schnee and seen it for himself, Adams could flesh out the mathematics of the scene.

A tidal wave of numbers was flowing over the Ardennes and into the Losheim Gap. All those scattered fixed islands of defense were being overrun. One after another his mind erased them. The Gap would logically belong to one German army group. North of the Gap a different army would be attacking. South of the Gap, toward Luxembourg City, a third one. It was only reasonable. And these pincers would close first around St. Vith. The numbers danced before him, as if on a screen. He thought about how many men Bradley had for reinforcements, how long it would take to bring them into line. He calculated how quickly Bradley could respond, and how fast the Germans could move their big tanks in the snow and the fog. He counted divisions, battalions, remembered weather forecasts, mentally penciled in bridges and logical places for fuel dumps to be.

When he finally looked away from the map, the G-2 office was deserted and he was alone.

# Six

In Versailles on the same morning of December 16, the Supreme Commander of the Allied Forces, Dwight Eisenhower, had just sat down to his correspondence. First on his list was an answer to a more-or-less humorous cable from the British Field Marshall Bernard Montgomery. Just before Operation Market Garden, Montgomery had bet Eisenhower five dollars that the war would be over by Christmas. Suddenly now Montgomery was dunning him for the money.

Doubtless Eisenhower paused a moment before answering. That the snobbish Montgomery looked on him with disdain was an open secret in Allied headquarters. Famously, Montgomery had remarked in earshot of a dozen senior officers, "Yes, Ike. Nice chap. No soldier." But Eisenhower's job was to manage egos as well as armies. There was no point in being on bad terms with the British. He took out his pen and scribbled, "Monty, I still have nine days!"

Then he turned to the next set of papers on his desk, which contained a brief and unexcited report of artillery and small arms fire in the Ardennes.

In Bastogne, her Luxembourg City idyll over, Annie March had just stepped out of the shower. Her hair was in a towel turban. Her clean fatigue pants were spread on the bed. The nurse she was bunking with had left her a cup of tepid coffee from the hotel dining room downstairs, and next to it a copy of that morning's *Stars & Stripes*. Still turbaned and wearing nothing else—Shaw said he liked her like that—she picked up the paper and quickly scanned it for news of the 101st. No news of it. No news of anything much. The Germans had launched a small spoiling attack east of the town of St. Vith. No one thought it would amount to anything.

In Paris, Martha Gellhorn had already been at her desk for an hour. This was her point of pride, her writing discipline. She liked to compare herself to the novelist Trollope, who could finish one novel and start another before breakfast. She wasn't writing a novel, however. She had already touched up an article on French politics for the *Times*. Now she pulled a packet of Hôtel Scribe stationery onto her desk and began to write a note to General Gavin of the 82nd Airborne, thanking him for taking her to the ballet last night—the rugged, much-decorated general was, to the wonder of his troops, a passionate *balletomane*—and also thanking him, coyly, for "the rest of the pleasures of the evening as well."

She liked Gavin. He was handsome, he made her laugh, and he wasn't above gossip. Last night he had told her that once in a meeting, Churchill said that General de Gaulle's perpetually "offended" expression made him look "like a female llama surprised in her bath." She signed her note "M" and wondered if she could possibly get Gavin's joke into print.

Out of the corner of her eye she saw her copy of the *New York Herald Tribune* slipped under the door. When she unfolded it to read, there was nothing important. On page three the Associated Press mentioned a brief local action in the Ardennes. She glanced at it, shrugged, and turned the page to a comic strip she liked, "Terry and the Pirates."

IN ST. VITH, ADAMS OPENED THE SCHOOLHOUSE DOOR ONTO THE most chaotic traffic jam he had ever seen, though far worse was soon to follow.

In the creeping pre-dawn haze, the gray town square, the main street, all the side streets and alleys—nothing but a snarl of cars, horns, jeeps, trucks, anti-tank guns, and hysterical civilians. Nobody was moving, everybody was shouting. A German shell exploded down the road, and despite the cold and fog a house burst into flame. *Anarchy*, Adams thought—Anarchy, the redheaded daughter of Mars. And despising anarchy and disorder, he pushed and elbowed his way along the sidewalk looking for his jeep. But when he reached the motor pool lot it was gone, of course, liberated, stolen. In its place stood an ancient wooden-wheeled farm wagon and a sway-backed horse with a mad look in its eye.

Ignoring the uproar around him, Adams sheltered inside a doorway and calculated possibilities. Back to Manderfeld was where he should go—the command post at Manderfeld was closer to the Gap, there he could find out enough to make a report to Eberhardt—but Manderfeld was eleven kilometers away. The mad horse whinnied and showed its teeth. *Shaw would hop on it*, Adams thought. He wouldn't wait for a jeep. Shaw would hop on it like a cowboy, gallop up the ridge, waving his vorpal sword, snicker-snack. Shaw wasn't here.

On the other side of the wagon a helmet popped up, then Sergeant Klippel's red face, then his arm waving Adams forward. At the back of an alley Klippel had confiscated a civilian Citroën even more ancient than the horse-drawn wagon, a battered green Deux-Chevaux with what seemed like a sewing machine for a motor and a gear stick that you pulled in and out like a trombone slide.

"Like old times, Major!"

He steered the car across somebody's back yard, swung onto the road toward Manderfeld, and grinned at Adams. "Fucking Wild West, Major!"

Afterwards, trying to organize for Martha's book what had happened, he found that all he could remember were moments, pictures. Martha made some comment about the Duke of Wellington's comparison of a ballroom dance to a battle—nobody ever saw the whole picture, only the dances you were part of. But a battlefield, Adams thought, was no ballroom.

What he remembered best was the first panorama at Manderfeld. It was still dark up on the Schnee when he returned—he saw with amazement that it was only 6:30—but down the hill the Germans came, stepping magically out of the fog. They moved in a slow, careful walk, not firing yet. The artificial moonlight cast down by the searchlights showed them clear and clean against the snow. Some wore American uniforms, others wore white camouflage sheets. To the left of the command post more came gliding gracefully down on skis. As Adams watched through his binoculars they swarmed over a farmhouse and went inside. Behind him the American colonel in charge said something to his radioman. A moment later one of their three anti-tank guns blasted the farmhouse to kindling. Then phosphorous grenades turned it into a torch.

After that—after that, he remembered wondering how you could have both smoke and fog at the same time. He remembered a tracer bullet, almost spent, hitting a tree beside him. The rear half stuck out from the bark and sputtered little red wisps like a

Roman candle. He remembered German bodies stacked up like cordwood in front a machine gun. He remembered watching terrified GIs flat on their bellies in the snow, weeping, vomiting. He saw one man, a coward, desperate to get out of the war, reach his arm around a tree and let a grenade explode in his hand.

Adams had never thought he would be craven like that in combat. He always thought he would be calm, analytic. But in fact, as the fighting around Manderfeld intensified, the orderly part of his nature went to ground. The lord of misrule in him took over and for an uncountable period of time he found himself metamorphosed from Horus to Hotspur, from Adams to Shaw.

Between strobic flashes of light and smoke, he ran to join Klippel's platoon, advancing uphill toward the descending Germans. There were thirty, forty of them running and dodging crazily, merrily behind the ridiculous little Citroën as it bounced over the snow. He saw Klippel firing his carbine from the window—it really was like the Wild West—he saw men firing from the hip as they walked. He saw bursts of red mist in the air, which he knew were the heads of soldiers, blown to blood. Minute by minute he saw more and still more Germans churning out of the forest, fewer and fewer American cowboys, fewer and fewer Americans at all.

After an hour the numbers were all wrong. The American colonel ordered a retreat to St. Vith, and he told Adams he should go to Bastogne, where the radios would work and he could call Versailles for reinforcements.

"It took me *two full days* to get there," Adams told Martha, later. "Except for the Germans shooting at me, I could have walked over the roofs of all the stalled cars and trucks heading out of the Ardennes and back toward Bastogne. But they were very much shooting at me, so I scrounged rides when I could, stopped when I had to. I was stuck half a day in a château in Clervaux, hiding in the basement with a bunch of clucking nuns. Most of the time I didn't know where I was. Apparently, it was the biggest, most chaotic retreat in army history."

Martha was writing fast in her notebook. "Eight thousand Americans surrendered on one day." She looked up. "Were you at Malmedy?"

Adams shook his head.

She wrote one more note, then sat back and studied him, expressionless. "Where was Shaw in all this?"

# Seven

Five days before Christmas, just before dawn, Annabella March stood in the snow and watched a hundred or so GIs carefully pulling condoms off the muzzles of their rifles.

It was seven in the morning, still half dark. The town a mile down the road was Luzery, little more than a crossroads north of Bastogne. The GIs belonged to the Second Battalion of the 506th Infantry, and they were dropping out of formation to dig foxholes and set up a defensive perimeter.

Annie steadied her camera and wondered if there was enough light for a photo of the condoms (though the chances of British *Vogue* running *that* were zero) and if the shutter would click in the cold. One of the GIs grinned at her and pointed to his boot tops, where he had tied two more of them to blouse his pant legs. Despite the cold she had to grin back. The troops used condoms to keep snow and mud out of their rifles, but it made an undeniably odd and racy sight, hundreds of the things hanging loosely over the rifle muzzles, flapping about to the rhythm of the march. *Eros and Thanatos*, she thought, as usual. She missed Shaw.

Ahead of her, the First and Third Battalions continued forward, bearing right on the road toward the next town of Noville, though in the poor light you could scarcely see the markers. It would be hard to know when they actually got to Noville, until they ran into the Germans, who were supposed to be swooping down toward them like Teutonic furies.

By a series of accidents and misunderstandings, Annie was one of exactly two journalists left in Bastogne—the other was a genial, avuncular middle-aged man named Fred McKenzie, who wrote for the Buffalo *Evening News*. Under the army's rules, she was allowed to go as far as Noville with the 506th, but if German artillery started coming in heavy, she was to leave lickety-split for the safety of Bastogne. Martha had been an excellent teacher. Annie had no intention of leaving.

For one thing, the battle for Bastogne was obviously going to be something no journalist could miss—as even a *Vogue* reporter could see on a map, Bastogne controlled all the roads west out of the Ardennes. And for another, somewhere among the ten thousand GIs now coming in from Luxembourg, somewhere in all those cheerful, condom-waving pink-cheeked American boys was the 506th of the 101st and Company D and John Michael Shaw.

Now she could hear gunfire from Luzery. Ahead of her the GIs began scattering into the ditches on either side of the road. Annie herself took shelter behind a tree and aimed the camera at the back of an elephant-hipped Sherman tank that was clanking and chuffing past. Then the tank stopped. The gunfire stopped. Everybody waited two, three minutes. When there was no more fire, the marching resumed.

At Luzery, incredibly, the town café was open, and since she couldn't fight and she wanted to warm her camera, she went inside and ordered a coffee. The café was empty. The *patronne* was of a silver-haired, grandmotherly age, wrapped in peasant black, faintly bewhiskered. She brought Annie a big bowl of coffee and a tiny pitcher of cream and sat down close beside her on the bench, silent, evidently just hungry for the company of a woman.

Together they watched the men going past the window, marching as to war.

Outside Noville about noon, Annie stopped walking and pulled her camera out of its bag. Off to one side of the road a jeep hung tilted precariously over a ditch. One wheel was suspended in air, spinning softly, quietly. You could barely hear it turning, even up close, over the boom of artillery ahead and the bark of rifles. The driver, a helmetless kid, was leaning sideways out of his seat at an angle that made his head loll over the ditch. The blood from his throat dripped steadily down to the ground, so much blood that the ditch ran red for a hundred yards.

Annie looked through her viewer. If it had been an exercise in composition, the little scene would have been striking—red blood over white snow, the angle of the jeep and the soldier's head, a distant stone bridge.

Her fingers were too cold to press the shutter. Or maybe it was her eyes. She lowered the camera and squatted on her heels in the snow while more soldiers tramped past her and disappeared over a rise. In retrospect, she thought, it may have been the words "*vengez-moi*" scratched in blood on the wall in Paris, at the Gestapo torture station. Or the dying soldier in Normandy, cut in half by shrapnel, intestines crawling like big red worms out of his torso, his pelvis and manhood torn away. Or the bald mother in Chartres. Or the dead boy in front of her right now. Or those things, all of them, in increments, bit by bit, sight by sight. "I belong to the school of no single explanation," her father used to say. But by now, after six months of it, Annie had lost all sense that the war was exciting, as the plucky nurses at Chartres had said, or fascinating or profound, like a Greek poem.

In Bastogne a nurse had told her that one of her boys had awoken suddenly and stared at her and said just one word, "Today." He died an hour later. Where was the meaning in that?

Where was Shaw?

NOVILLE WAS A TYPICAL ARDENNES TOWN—A HAPHAZARD assortment of sixty or seventy gray fieldstone buildings that looked as if they had simply dropped out of the sky onto a flat spot in the road.

It had a church, of course, and if its squat Romanesque architecture bore no resemblance at all to the two noble, cloud-piercing spires at Chartres, like all churches it was still an observation point. Like a bridge, it connected two worlds. When she reached the top of the bell tower, she found herself overlooking the main road north to Malmedy, the road and the fields and the whole black and white carpet of countryside below, where another battle, probably to be described in the great sweep of things as "minor," was about to begin.

*From a suitable distance*, she thought, *maybe anything makes sense*. Without the distance of a map you wouldn't understand that Italy was shaped like a boot and Spain like a shield. Without the distance of a map you wouldn't understand why Hitler's massive attack west, driving toward Antwerp like a gigantic fist, was being called "the Bulge." Without some kind of distance you couldn't imagine the line running across the map, the fat black arrow that showed where the Germans would come on their way through Noville, or the neatly drawn arc of foxholes and gun emplacements that the Americans had drawn across the white fields to stop them and slaughter them. Of course, the map didn't care.

But these Germans were coming from Malmedy, and no map or observation post in the world could show what had happened in Malmedy five days earlier. There was a limit to what distance could anesthetize.

By now everybody knew the story. In Malmedy, on the second day of the Ardennes offensive, an elite SS panzer unit had herded a hundred and thirty American prisoners into a field. For a few minutes the Americans simply stood in rows, arms held up in the air, while the SS troopers walked among them taking wristwatches, rings, cigarettes, anything they fancied. An American officer protested and a German simply shot him dead on the spot. Then a German half-track with a machine gun came up the road and stopped opposite the field.

*How long did it seem*, Annie wondered, *how long had it seemed to the prisoners as they watched the half-track move into position? How many breaths could they take before the machine gun suddenly opened fire and they went down, falling over row after row, reeds bending before a red wind?*

All told, perhaps a dozen of the one hundred and thirty prisoners managed to escape in the middle of the massacre, or played dead well enough to fool the SS troops who walked around the field finishing the job. An American medical aide asked to tend to one of the wounded, and a German sergeant allowed him to bandage his patient. Then he shot them both. For hours afterward, to amuse themselves, passing Germans would stop and fire a few rounds into the mass of bodies left unburied in the snow.

Annie peered over the rim of the bell tower and listened to the artillery. The German shells were coming closer now, but still landing well clear of the crossroads where the church was located. She snapped a few more pictures. She wasn't afraid, but somehow her heart wasn't in it. She thought of how John Michael Shaw had captured eleven Germans in Normandy and let them live. After Malmedy—and every GI in Europe knew about Malmedy—would he still let them live? Or had time made a stone of his heart?

The bell tower steps were littered with broken glass. A dead pigeon lay with its head at a broken angle, not unlike the soldier in the jeep. Annie gathered her camera and pack and started back down, thinking that she had seen enough. She wanted Shaw.

# Eight

SHAW WAS TWELVE KILOMETERS AWAY, IN A FIELD EAST OF BAStogne, somewhere near a village called Wardin, although his map was so wet and dirty that he thought he could be anywhere.

"Eat some snow."

He crouched beside a foxhole and held out a handful of snow. Driskell looked up at him suspiciously.

"Your mouth's dry, isn't it? My mouth always gets dry."

Driskell scraped a little snow from Shaw's glove and licked at it.

"I should have joined the navy, I guess," Shaw said. "'Water, water everywhere.'"

Driskell turned his eyes away, toward a distant ridge, and seemed to burrow even deeper into the foxhole. He was shivering uncontrollably under his field jacket, and no wonder. The last time Shaw had checked, the temperature was ten below zero. They had left Mourmelon-le-Grand three days ago in such a hurry that nobody in Company D, nobody in the entire battalion, had proper winter coats. Shaw watched Driskell shiver and kicked himself for having made the kid throw away his sister's sweater.

Driskell was from Georgia, he remembered. He had probably never been so cold in his life.

"Plenty of snow to eat," Shaw said fatuously. He patted Driskell's shoulder and started off in his Groucho Marx walk for the next foxhole. For the next ten minutes he moved that way from foxhole to foxhole, checking on his men. Sometimes he made them eat a little snow, because most canteens were frozen solid. Sometimes he checked to see that they were all wearing multiple pairs of socks and had gloves.

"Fucking mother hen," the First Platoon sergeant said. "Sir." But he took the hint and began double-checking the foxholes himself. At the end of his perimeter, where Company D's line stopped, Shaw loped back half a mile to the battalion command post to go over his orders. On the way he passed a "snatch squad" coming back—a patrol sent out to capture a German to interrogate. Their prisoner was evidently an SS trooper, because they had taken off his shoes and socks and were making him walk barefooted across the snow. When his feet were numb enough, they would be amputated. After Malmedy that was standard practice. If the prisoner happened to be caught wearing US Army boots, he was simply shot.

Shaw tried to have no feelings about that.

At the command post—a farmer's kitchen table—all four captains gathered around their colonel. *His* map was still clean enough to show what they already knew—Bastogne sat at the convergence of five major and three minor highways, and Bastogne was surrounded. It was a stubborn island of resistance that three huge panzer divisions were trying to flow around, like water around a rock. Anybody could see that unless the Germans took Bastogne, they couldn't push their bulge all the way to Antwerp. So until Eisenhower poured in enough reinforcements to save the city, the 101st's job was just to be expendable, a forward human wall, slowly crumbling.

"Everybody stays in line," the colonel said. "It's supposed to clear off enough tomorrow for air support." Nobody bothered to look out the farmer's window. There was no sky, only fog and blankets of gray clouds. No planes were going to fly tomorrow. "Everybody stays in line," the colonel said. "Because the Krauts are probably going to attack right through where we are. They want to take Wardin and have supper in Bastogne tonight, and we're in their way." He sat down and started to draw arrows on the map.

"SS?" one of the captains asked.

"*Volksgrenadiers*. Not nearly as bad. You're gonna love 'em." The colonel stabbed his pencil stub on the map. "D Company's right in their way, east of this road, so Battalion's sending some anti-tank guns to back them up. Maybe they'll get here in time, maybe they won't." He drew a circle on the map. "D Company," he said and blew his lower lip like a walrus. "Bull's eye. You hit the jackpot, Captain Shaw."

WHEN HE HEARD THE FIRST THUMP OF ARTILLERY, IT WAS TWO-thirty in the afternoon, although the fog was so thick and the clouds so dark that Shaw could barely read his watch. He thought of Thucydides and the night battle at Epipolae when "ignorant armies clashed by night," the poet said, and he thought he was an over-educated Harvard asshole, and he thought he needed to keep close to Driskell, because the kid was scared and cold and Shaw still felt guilty about the sweater.

Company D had dug in along a humpbacked ridge several hundred yards long. Behind them a narrow road ran north-south to Bastogne. In front of them lay a snow-covered field, at least a hundred yards deep. And beyond it was a cultivated grove of the kind Shaw had seen all over northern France—a dark forest of pines whose lower limbs had all been trimmed away, who knew why? In theory, with the limbs trimmed away, they should see any enemy troops advancing through the forest. In reality, they could only see fog.

The artillery came closer, slowly finding their range, throwing up geysers of snow and shrapnel in the field. Yard by yard the shells walked toward the foxholes. Already the familiar noise had begun in Shaw's head, familiar since Normandy, the shattering *kee-whump* that made him feel as if his head were in a bell hammered by giants. And because the sounds were always the same, then there would come the devil's staccato of men screaming and motors grinding and the *pop-pop-pop* of soldiers at play.

But the colors were different this time. Normandy had been summer, bright, green, a yellow French sun in an endless blue sky. The Netherlands autumnal brown and warm. The Ardennes was *winter,* hard winter—the pine forest was black, the snow around him was white, the fog settling down on them was gray. He had the bizarre illusion that he was crouching on a strip of film in an old black-and-white movie.

Two of his men on the right were standing in their foxholes, urinating on their M-1s, which was what you did to unfreeze the trigger. Uselessly, Shaw yelled at them to get down. At the same moment the first Germans emerged out of the fog.

They came forward at their characteristic slow walk, silent black figures tramping across the snow. The artillery stopped firing to let them attack and suddenly all Shaw could hear was the distant crunch of boots on snow coming forward. It was strange—when Americans attacked they yelled and ran and plunged ahead like madmen. But Germans came on at a measured pace, rank after rank, wave after wave, somehow more frightening than all the "Geronimos:" and "Hubba-hubbas" in the world.

Afterwards, as always, he had little sense of the time that had passed. They beat back the first wave of Germans and then there was a pause—how long he couldn't say. He remembered climbing out of his foxhole and going up and down his line again, checking his people. The company intellectual, Nagle, he discovered, had been shot in the shoulder but refused to leave. He was propped in his hole cradling his rifle and drinking brandy from a canteen because, he said, "Water freezes at thirty-two degrees, but it has to go down to *twenty* below for fucking alcohol, sir. You should try it." Shaw took a swallow and went on down the line until he came to Driskell.

The boy was crouched in his foxhole in a fetal position, noiseless except for his shivering. Shaw knelt at the edge of the hole and looked toward the fog-shrouded, smoke-shrouded forest, which was quiet for now, holding its breath.

*You notice the dumbest things,* he thought, *while people are trying to kill you.* A few yards in front of Driskell's foxhole burnt powder had left elegant fan-shaped marks on the snow. Those were from artillery shells that struck the ground at a flat angle. Farther away, mortar shells had made very different circular powder marks, with delicate ragged edges. Seen from above, they must have created a beautiful pointillist pattern. Over-education was keeping him sane. Adams, he remembered, liked pointillism because out of its random dots and colors an order always emerged. But to Shaw, its patterns were precarious, like all order, unstable, poised to dissolve at any moment.

"Is it over yet?"

Shaw climbed down in the foxhole with Driskell and tried to talk with him about football, the Georgia Tech team, Alabama. But at some point, just as the boy was calming down, the second wave of the attack began, and this time there were tanks.

# Nine

THE SIEGE OF BASTOGNE BEGAN ON DECEMBER 20 AND WAS TO last until December 27, when Patton's Third Army arrived from Luxembourg to lift it.

If Annie had been more literary—if she had been Martha— she might have compared that endless week to the horrors of the siege of Troy.

But she was too cold and hungry to try to call up ancient history. After Noville, she had hurried back to Bastogne just hours before the German armies completed their encirclement and sealed it off. "Bastogne's the hole in the doughnut," one of the American officers told her, but Annie thought that was a poor image (Martha would have called it stupid). Bastogne was a hard kernel surrounded by a ring of paratroopers, the 101st Airborne— *her* paratroopers, *her* Shaw—which was day by day falling back, falling apart. The Germans were a circle closing around the ring.

Of course, people told themselves, there was always the chance that hunger and cold would destroy the city before the Germans did. Bastogne normally had a population of four thousand, but as thousands of refugees streamed in from the countryside, as stretcher after stretcher of bleeding GIs was carried in, the city had almost ceased to function. By night, civilians huddled in cellars and listened to the whine and boom of artillery. By day, they crowded into one of the town's three churches and waited as best they could, dreaming of food.

On December 22 two things happened. First, under a white flag of truce, the Germans sent a delegation to point out that the city was doomed. They demanded immediate surrender. The American commander, General Anthony McAuliffe, sent back a one-word reply: "Nuts."

Second, that same day somebody found seven tons of flour and two tons of tinned biscuits stored in the local Boys' Seminary. And then somebody else found enough coal at the railroad station to heat the tiny Hôtel LeBrun, where General McAuliffe sat by his radios and cursed the fog and the clouds that kept the Allied planes from dropping supplies.

Food and coal. But nobody found medicine. Bastogne had two regular doctors, the army had six more, and three surgeons— far too few for so many sick and wounded, even if there had been bandages and sulfur and morphine. Out on the doughnut's perimeters, the 101st was outnumbered by the Germans five to one. Ammunition was fast disappearing. Most of the men had been hurried up from Mourmelon-le-Grand without enough helmets, without real winter clothing. The other journalist in Bastogne, Fred McKenzie, told Annie that on the way north one of the battalions raided a hat factory and all of the soldiers had come out of it wearing derbies and fedoras. Annie tried to picture Shaw in a derby and first laughed, then cried.

When she couldn't crowd into the radio room herself and send out bulletins to the wire services, she tried to make herself useful by working with the nurses. Nobody, of course, could be evacuated, so the wounded literally piled up. In the Sarma Department Store more than a hundred overflow patients lay on blankets on the floor. In a church by the town center Annie found so many men on the floor that the medics had to step over and around them. When the church was filled, the wounded were placed in a neighboring garage, lying on beds of sawdust because blankets were scarce.

Annie loved the nurses. Like all of the other nurses she had met, these were funny and sweet and dying of grief on the inside. One trio on the same duty shift invited her to bunk with them and told her their three unbreakable rules. First, if anybody received powdered Jell-O from home, it had to be given to the Gut Wound Ward at once. Second, all soap from home was to be shared. Third, if they were at a party—and there had been parties just weeks earlier—and one girl had a nice dress, she could only wear it two hours. Then she had to disappear and let another girl wear it. They called it their Cinderella rule.

On Christmas Eve the Sarma Store was bombed and all three nurses were killed.

In the cold many corpses simply froze and hardened. Outside the Graves Registration tent Annie took a photograph of a truck full of bodies like that brought in from the field. Two GIs began to unload the truck by simply tossing the bodies down like sticks of lumber. Annie raised her camera.

A paratrooper with a bloody bandage over one eye walked over the truck and pulled out his pistol. He aimed it at the soldiers and said quietly, "Do that once more, and I'll blow your fucking heads off." They stared at the pistol and then lowered the next body carefully to a stretcher.

Once, Annie ran into B.T. Adams, who had stayed in Bastogne and taken over most of McAuliffe's intelligence operations. He was brilliant at it, people said. His interrogations of German prisoners gave the American artillery key targets to fire at, key bridges to block. Part of Annie cynically wondered if B.T., now rigidly military, had volunteered to stay because he saw an opportunity for yet another promotion. But she was glad to see him anyway, and they shared a bowl of cold beet soup in the basement of the Seminary and talked about the siege and Harvard and Paris, and just a little about Shaw.

On Christmas morning she was in a corner of the Hôtel LeBrun lobby, scribbling a story, when Fred McKenzie found her.

"Your boy's in the First Battalion?" He plopped down in the chair opposite her and pulled sympathy into his face.

Annie nodded. "506th."

"That's the one." Fred shook his head. "They were in a terrible fight a couple of days back, at Wardin. Tanks."

Annie held her breath. You heard unbearable things about infantry and tanks.

"What company?"

She told him and he smoothed a packet of mimeographed sheets of paper on the table between them, the after-action report for First Battalion. Annie went straight to the last sheet, which was the casualty list. She read it three times. She couldn't find Shaw's name.

Then she realized that Fred was reading the citations page out loud, and after a moment she heard "Captain J. M. Shaw"—trapped under a tank, the dry military report said. Trapped under a tank—Annie closed her eyes. Germans were notorious for rolling their tanks back and forth over a foxhole, crushing the men beneath into jelly. "Trapped under a German Mark IV twenty-seven-ton tank, Captain J. M. Shaw fought his way out and rescued a wounded private named Driskell. He then destroyed the tank with a bazooka and stormed two others, destroying them and killing at least a dozen Germans singlehandedly." She was crying too much to listen anymore.

"Silver Star again, for sure," Fred said.

Annie turned away toward the window. She saw an ambulance, a frozen sky, two GIs walking by. The soldiers were unshaven, dirty; they had vacant looks in their eyes that would never go away. She knew she should be proud, but she could only think of John Michael huddled in a foxhole, trapped under the sharp, muddy, indifferent metal slats of the tank treads. Dirt would crumble down the edges of the foxhole. The roar and clank of the engine would be deafening, the smell of exhaust fumes blasting into his face. And Driskell, whoever he was, covering his head with his arms, burrowing and shaking into the mud. Shaw killed a dozen men. A good soldier has to be filled with hate.

"Got away without a scratch," Fred said admiringly.

Annie shook her head. What was the phrase her father liked? In your deep heart's core? In her deep heart's core, she knew he was wounded.

# Ten

ALL THROUGH THE NIGHT OF DECEMBER 26 IT WAS TOO COLD TO
sleep, too cold even for fog.

Shaw spent it in a three-man trench with two of his sergeants,
arms wrapped around each other for body heat. They were dug
in again somewhere northwest of Wardin, a modest half-mile
counter advance after the tank attack. But every foot of it had
been paid for in blood.

Throughout the long night, Shaw shivered and gnawed at a
chocolate bar and listened to the screams and sobs of the wounded
out in the fields. The German cannon fire never stopped. Sometimes, when shells burst high enough, the light revealed hundreds
of bodies out in no man's land where even the medics couldn't go.
There were so many bodies, so many dead men, that Shaw began
to hate them.

Shaw twisted in the trench and thought he could write a little college theme on the subject of dead bodies in the Ardennes.
Dead Germans' faces, for instance, took on a strange green color;
nobody knew why. Dead Americans often had faces that were
burgundy red, because it was so goddam cold that the blood in
the capillaries instantly froze. Sometimes his paratroopers set up

frozen bodies to draw enemy fire. Sometimes they stacked German bodies like planks to make a little fort.

The worst body? Two days ago, pushing out of Wardin, they found an American who had been killed and frozen rigid. The Germans propped him up and stiffened his right arm and ran a telephone wire through his outstretched fingers. German humor, the saying went, is no laughing matter.

At dawn the artillery bombardments grew heavier. At eight-thirty Shaw made his way back to the battalion command post and found himself standing in front of a map, as usual. It was odd, when he landed in Normandy, he could read Greek and Latin without a dictionary, and now he had forgotten every word of them, but he could read a map like a lover's face.

This one was easy and ominous. C and D Companies were strung out along the edge of a snow-covered pasture. Beyond the pasture the land began to undulate like the ocean, waves of rounded, hump-backed hills alternating with steep valleys. Farming country, winding roads and stray farmhouses everywhere. The artillery pounding their pasture was probably three valleys over and a little to the north, but nobody could say for sure.

"Sound and Flash team," Shaw said, and his major nodded and looked first at the captain from C Company and then at Shaw.

"Tag," he told Shaw. "You're it."

THE SOUND AND FLASH TECHNIQUE WAS DEVISED BY COMBAT engineers to locate enemy gun and mortar emplacements. It was an "in-your-head" mathematical exercise that would have pleased B.T. Adams—the engineers crawled or dodged as close as possible to the front line, then went farther. When they reached a workable point, they set up microphones and then laid wires all the way back to their own lines. Once at their command post, by coordinating sounds and flashes, they could calculate where the guns were.

Because the engineers carried no weapons, only their microphones and heavy spools of wire, infantry had to go along to guard them.

At nine o'clock, light snow began to fall and the morning light dimmed to a thin, watery gray, the color of ice. Shaw assembled First Platoon on the crest of a hill and tracked the engineers through his binoculars. When they were a hundred yards to his right—*a hundred yards*, he thought, *the length of a football field*; it was how Americans measured distance—he hustled his people forward, spread out in a wing, a fucking mother hen.

There was no need to tell his people to walk carefully. For one thing, artillery was still booming ahead of them, exploding behind them. For another, the Germans had been in the same area for two full days before they pulled back, and they had undoubtedly booby-trapped some of the bodies still lying on the snow. Only medics and fools touched a corpse.

The mines were worse. Shaw had no idea how many different kinds of mines the Nazi genius had contrived. But two of them scared him silly. One was called a shoe mine—a narrow wooden box, like a shoebox, with a slightly raised lid. The slightest pressure of a boot would set it off. They put it under six inches of snow.

The other mine the Americans called the "Castrator"—a tube about the size of a fountain pen, buried in the ground pointing straight up. If you stepped on it, a projectile came slicing up through your foot. And *up* and *up*.

He thought of Malmedy and what the Germans were capable of. He thought of the unnatural way he was walking, M-1 rifle at the ready, half on his toes, dreading every step. He was weaving around possible mine sites, corpses, like a dancer, looking for people to kill. He had been a lovable little boy, his mother had said so. He never liked loud noises, never played soldier or cowboys and Indians. Where had the little boy gone? He felt numb, inside and out.

THE FOURTH AND FINAL MOMENT THAT WOULD DESTROY FORever Annabella March's moral universe came at nine twenty-two that morning.

The engineers to Shaw's right had just reached the top of a ridge and started to plant their microphones. For the next three or four minutes they would be completely in the open, clearly visible against the snow. Close behind them, over the *whump* and crash of artillery, Shaw motioned his men to the ground and peered over the ridge.

Below him, on the left, ran a narrow curving road. At the center of his field of vision the road bent hard left, around a grove of pines, and disappeared. A stone farmhouse sat just before the bend, and to Shaw's amazement, smoke was drifting out of a chimney. He dug his chin into the snow and aimed the M-1 at the farmhouse door. Germans in the farmhouse? Civilians? Off to the right the engineers were slipping and sliding along a wide white slope, perfect targets. He must have glanced at them, but he had no sense of it. He flicked snowflakes out of his eyes. He listened for the charming sound of bullets. He balanced the farmhouse door on his barrel and waited.

"Fuck."

The man on Shaw's right came half to his knees, and an instant later Shaw heard it too, even over the artillery, the ratcheting whine of an engine. Just beyond the bend in the road, behind the trees, a German half-track had rattled to a halt. When he slid a few feet to his right Shaw could see it plainly, though as far as he could tell the Germans couldn't yet see him or the sound and flash team. Through his binoculars Shaw counted a dozen men in the back, holding their rifles vertically, like Roman spears. In front, above the driver's cab, he saw the mounted machine gun that would slaughter his engineers. The gunner himself was almost invisible behind a high metal shield. The driver was wrestling with the gears.

The artillery kept booming, but in Shaw's mind everything went silent. He felt his men's faces turning toward him, questioning. He saw the second hand on his watch stop, as if to hold its breath. If the half-track stayed where it was for another minute, the engineers would be out of sight and safe. But if it lurched forward a few yards….Beyond the next ridge another thunderous barrage shook the sky like a blanket. Give him one minute. His people needed one more minute. And the farmhouse door opened.

Shaw would never know how long it took for the door to open completely and the little girl to step out. She was blonde, like so many Belgians, eleven or twelve years old he would have guessed. She wore a light blue jacket and a dark beret. There was far too much artillery noise for the Germans to hear her. She walked toward the bend in the road, waving at the half-track and pointing her arm uphill toward the engineers.

The trees still blocked her. The shielded gunner still couldn't see her, not right away, not in the eternity it took for Shaw's rifle to move an inch to the left. Wilcox's face appeared in the falling snow, then Driskell's, then Annie's. Then the girl's face. It was meet, right and his bounden duty. And there was no health in him. His finger began to squeeze the trigger, just the way they teach you, just the way that had become second nature to him, the squeeze, the jolt, the sudden bright red blossom of blood.

When the engineers reached cover, Shaw crawled backwards down the ridge, past the eyes of his people, past the gaping mouths, past Nagle, past his favorite sergeant. Then he stood up and dropped his rifle in the snow and walked away.

# Epilogue

## Paris, December 5, 1945

"He's coming," she said.

At the far end of the Pont Neuf, from the Left Bank side, Shaw slowly came into focus, or Shaw's ghost. It was hard to be sure. He was a shifting, indecisive shadow.

Annie stepped cautiously on to the sidewalk. After a moment's pause she began to walk, even more slowly than Shaw, toward the dividing point of the bridge, which was not quite the center, the little park on the right side where the big worried equestrian statue of Henry IV peered upstream, studying the future.

Her caution didn't surprise Adams. He knew that Annie had already seen Shaw before tonight—three times, according to Martha Gellhorn—but Shaw had sent her away each time, more miserable than before. He can't live with himself, Martha had said. So he couldn't live with her either.

Adams stepped out onto the sidewalk, too, and stopped. He made a point of looking straight at Shaw, not to either side, not over his shoulder. There were no cars now, and no pedestrians. The bridge was abnormally quiet and empty, and Adams guessed that Shaw was thinking about that. Do not, he had warned himself, underestimate Shaw's intelligence. The army had arrested him right on the battlefield, after he had thrown down his rifle and walked away, and when the Battle of the Bulge moved east, they had hurried him off to a cell in the "Disciplinary Training Center"—i.e., deserter's prison—near Le Mans. Four days after that, and the army still had no idea how, he escaped.

Annie glanced back at him. Then she broke into a run and threw herself into Shaw's arms, so hard Adams could hear their bodies meeting, with a sob anybody in the world could have heard.

Suddenly Adams had a hundred eyes, like Argus in the myth. He could see Annie's head buried in Shaw's neck; he could see Shaw himself, his brow, his hair now almost silver in the snow. Even under her bulky coat he could see Annie March's figure, the erotic curve of her right hip, and he felt the bitter copper taste in your mouth when you've lost forever what you wanted. He could see the faint opening to their left, where the place Dauphine began, and down below the waist-high balustrades, flickers of light riding the black current of the river. He could see the dark silhouettes of the buildings behind him, the Samaritaine department store, the massed shoulders of the Louvre. In front, through the snow and mist, he could see the distant world of the Left Bank, shivering. It had been colder in the Ardennes, but the same snow, the same bleak air. He wondered what it would be like to cry with a hundred eyes.

Annie had finally released Shaw and looked back. Adams started forward. When he had almost reached them, she took a few steps over to the curb to give them space. *The Pont Neuf is seventy-two feet wide*, Adams thought, *with unusually spacious side-walks. And 761 feet long*, he thought pointlessly.

"B.T.," Shaw said quietly.

Adams nodded, which was stupid, and then in a rush of three more steps, angry no more, reached his oldest friend, his Harvard twin, John Michael Shaw the Deserter.

It was a shorter embrace than Adams had expected, and harder. He pulled back an arm's length and shook his head. "You look good," he said.

When Shaw said nothing—"I told Annie I had to see you. We need to get you back."

Shaw's grin had always been something to see—boyish, joyous—but not tonight. "You look good, too. Major." A long, frozen pause. "You know, that's not the Seine down there," he said.

"No?"

"It's the River Styx."

Of course, he would have a goddam Latin reference, Adams thought, of course he would. In the *Aeneid* the River Styx divided the world of the living from the world of the dead. Shaw's classical shorthand put them each in their separate places.

"You have to come back, my old friend. I can help, *we* can help." A sidelong glance at Annie.

"B.T., you know what I did."

Adams knew what he had done. The after-action report said the girl was eleven. The engineers had escaped unscratched, the sound and flash had been a terrific success, uncountable GI lives were saved. In his mind Adams was arguing the case brilliantly, making his old roommate come around and see reason, just the way they had done centuries ago at Harvard, bullshitting, growing up together. But in reality he was simply standing there, silent for once. He can't live with himself, Martha had said. Or anyone else. Ever. Adams looked over at Annie.

Annie returned his look, sober, expressionless. She had long ago stopped crying, months ago, after the first time she found him back in the lawless warrens of the place d'Italie, where the black marketers and deserters and mad gangsters had created a kind of no man's land for the hopeless. War held up to a mirror.

"Bullets can't go backward," Shaw said softly. "Time can't go backward."

The Pont Neuf was eerily quiet. The sky had stopped whispering, the river had gone silent. She could hear every word. She had always liked B.T., she thought. She admired his loyalty to his old friend, but he wasn't like Shaw and he didn't understand.

"There'd be a trial," B.T. was saying. "A court martial. There'd have to be."

"There's already been a trial," Shaw said.

"You've got a duty to turn yourself in."

"*Got*," Shaw said, "the word that ate the English language." Just for a moment, both of them smiled at the joke, and, just for a moment, Annie's nerves relaxed, tension went out of the air. Then everything went wrong.

"Did you bring the MPs?" Shaw asked.

Adams looked down at his feet, then up.

"Where are they?"

Adams's head half-turned, back toward the Right Bank end of the bridge.

"You didn't know where she was bringing you, so I assume they followed you, what in—jeeps?"

"Jeeps."

"Well," Shaw said, almost conversationally, "you've got a duty, too. 'Arrest the war criminal, bring him in.' What's your signal?"

Adams shook his head.

"A kiss on my cheek?"

Annie's heart stopped. Annie's breath stopped.

Adams said, "I hold my left arm out straight and the MPs come."

Shaw smiled at Annie with infinite tenderness. Then he turned back and looked with infinite kindness at Adams, because Shaw, as Annie had always known, was the twin with the capacity to love. "Then do it," he said, and turned his back and started to walk away.

*If Adams raised his arm,* Annie thought, but the thought went nowhere. Adams's arm stayed by his side. He watched his friend's back growing smaller and smaller, and then he too turned and started to walk away, back to the other end of the bridge, the other side.

Annie stood where she was in the snow. A voice called something. But it wasn't Shaw's voice, so she ignored it. The snow was falling faintly. The snowflakes were flecks of light falling out of the sky, faintly falling, and then dissolving in the dark water and disappearing, crossing like everything else in life from one world to another.

# Note

For their kindness and encouragement I'm grateful to John Lescroart, B.J. Robbins, Andrew Rosenheim, and William Wood. And always and ever to Brookes Byrd.

It would be impossible to recite all the books and conversations that I have drawn on for details and information. I should mention, however, Cornelius Ryan's remarkable *A Bridge Too Far* and John Toland's moving *Battle: The Story of the Bulge.* Of recent books on the period, I am particularly indebted to *Snow and Steel: The Battle of the Bulge 1944-45* by Peter Caddick-Adams. I cannot recommend too highly the four volumes of combat memoirs by Donald R. Burgett, the best such personal history I know and the most valuable source I used. The second volume concerns Operation Market Garden, the third the battle for Bastogne. I have also pored over Martha Gellhorn's wonderful stories and war dispatches, sometimes quoted from them, and tried to capture her voice (her interaction with the fictional Annie is mostly my own doing). Unless they are obvious historical figures—e.g., Montgomery—the other principal characters are fiction.

In writing I had constantly in mind my friend Burnett Miller, 1923-2018, who won the Silver Star and the Purple Heart at the Battle of the Bulge.

# About the Author

Max Byrd is the author of many bestselling historical novels, including *Jefferson, Grant, The Paris Deadline,* and *The Sixth Conspirator.* His detective fiction has won the Shamus Award. He lives in northern California and plays a mean ukulele.